The Alchemist Royal

(A Courtier's Fall)

by **Anne Stevens**

Book Seven in the Tudor Crimes Series

Dedicated to my best friend, for her support, and encouragement.

Foreword

*

The year 1533 dawns on an England that is yet to wake up to the immense upheavals that lie ahead. King Henry has, without a word of warning, gone through a form of wedding ceremony in the Port of Calais, and returns to his realm with his new wife, Anne Boleyn.

They wed in England, officially, on the 25th day of January, 1533 to a somewhat mixed reception from the populace.

The keys to the kingdom seem to be within her grasp, and it only remains to be seen how she will respond to her new found status. Thomas Cromwell countenances a firm, but benign hand, gently guiding Henry, rather than attempting to bully him into her ways of doing things.

The marriage, though yet to be made official, with a visit to Westminster for the great bishops to sanctify it, is like a weapon placed in the hands of those who do not know how best to wield it.

Thomas Boleyn, the father of the new dynasty, immediately declares himself to be the Earl of Wiltshire, and affects the title of 'Monsignour', to raise him above lesser nobles, such as Norfolk, and Suffolk. His son, George, is soon to find himself with almost continuous access to both the king, and his sister, and his standing amongst the court 'braves' will never be higher than it is now.

The King's Oath of Allegiance is making its steady, but unstoppable, way into the English statute books, and will help drive a wedge between kings, and commoners, that will culminate in civil war, and tear the country apart. In the short term it will allow for the swift and certain removal of any who oppose the new regime.

Thomas Cromwell, and Queen Anne, once allies, are estranged over how the vast confiscated wealth of the Roman church is to be spent, and pass their days trying to win some small advantage in the struggle.

For Anne, it is about power, but for the Privy Councillor, it is much more. If the new found wealth is used well, it will benefit the entire realm, and make England the greatest amongst the great of Europe.

He realises that Anne wants to take another path, and so understands that he is becoming locked in a life or death struggle with the queen, and that there can be but one victor.

News of Queen Anne's pregnancy moves her into the ascendancy, and all at Austin Friars hold their breaths in trepidation. For once she has a son to show Henry... a legitimate heir to the throne of England... Anne Boleyn's power will become absolute, and her enemies must either bend the knee to her, or perish.

Still, everyday life must go on, and Mistress Miriam Draper spends her time between building up her mercantile empire, and trying to keep Thomas Cromwell well fed, and cared for...

1   The Waiting

"What is it now?" The girl curtseys, and holds out her basket, as if in explanation. Thomas Cromwell sighs, and puts down his penning knife. The sun is already up, and he has yet to start the day's work. "Where are you from, child?"

"Draper's House, if you please, Master Tom," the girl replies, adding a second curtsey. "Mistress Miriam says I'm not to leave until you've eaten something."

"Away with you, girl," Cromwell barks, "before I eat *you*!"

"Mistress says you can be an old bear, and I was to bid you cease your noise, and eat. Look see, there is a custard, and some fresh bread rolls with cheese and…"

"Enough!" Cromwell stands, crosses the room, and takes the basket. He tries to shoo the girl away, but she stands her ground. At last, he snatches up the custard pie, and takes a bite. It is delicious, and he crams the remainder into his mouth, and chews. "There. Tell your mistress that I have eaten."

"Good job," the girl says, and turns to leave.

"Stay a moment," Cromwell says. "How is little Gwyllam?"

"Running us all ragged, sir," the girl tells him, with a happy smile. "Mistress says you should visit more often."

"I will," Cromwell says, waving the girl away. "Leave the food on the table. It will save me a visit to my own kitchen."

The girl finally leaves, and Cromwell returns

to the task in hand. He is trying to write a plea in mitigation for some northerners, who say that the making, and the taking of oaths is against their religious beliefs. They quote from a Tyndale bible, and he fears for their safety. The king has no love for the man, and believes him to be against the monarchy.

"He is against stupidity," Cromwell mutters, and picks up his quill once more. "Is it not enough to rule, without being constantly pandered to?"

"You called, master?" Rafe, never far away these days, is in the door. "Can I be of service?"

"You are supposed to be the king's man," Cromwell tells him. "Who is advising him so badly these days?"

"George Boleyn is always there," Rafe replies. "Then the *monsignour* struts about like a peacock, demanding his rights and uttering rubbish into the king's ear."

"He wants to burn some townspeople, up in Carlisle."

"Ah, that will be Boleyn senior, I fear," Rafe says. "He has fallen out with Harry Percy over something, and causes trouble in his lands, whenever he can. Henry thinks it all a great jest."

"What, that men burn?" Cromwell shakes his head.

"That Lord Percy, and old Tom Boleyn, fight like cat and dog," Rafe explains. "He thinks of nothing beyond the present, not now he has his precious son on the way."

"Yes, that was quick work," Cromwell says. He still scolds himself for not acting sooner when he had the chance. Before Christmas, he could have brought the Boleyn clan down, but he left it too late, and they flourish now, like a tree in full blossom. "I hear that Queen Anne prays thrice a day for a male heir."

"I pay the bishop to pray *four* times a day that it is a girl," Rafe says, and they both laugh. It is a light moment in an otherwise dark day.

"What am I to do about these people?" Cromwell waves at the document on his desk. "Must they burn?"

"*Monsignour* wants Carlisle," says Rafe. "So, he stirs up dissent, to show Percy up for the fool he is."

"Then there is our answer," Cromwell replies. "We must stop poor Harry Percy being a fool. Have him put an order of restraint on Thomas Boleyn, saying he is fomenting sedition. Have our people draft it, and make sure Boleyn hears of it."

"He will be horrified." Rafe knows the power of fear, and the idea that Henry might hear of it, will scare Boleyn. "I suspect he will run to me, as Henry's pet lawyer."

"Then you must advise him to be wary. Have him withdraw his threat against Lord Percy, and have the duke write to Henry, confirming that all who must, will swear the new oath." Cromwell nods at his own cleverness. "Warn Thomas Boleyn that there is room at the king's table for all, and that upsetting the other lords will do him no good. Tell him I said so."

"He will hate you."

"He already does."

"Then he will hate you more."

"I have a strong back," Cromwell tells his

protegé. "Let them all hate me, as long as I do right."

"Queen Anne also wants the little princess declared a bastard."

"I was expecting as much," Tom Cromwell replies. "What does Henry think about that?"

"I fear he will agree." Rafe spends a lot of his time close to the king, and picks up almost his every nuance. "Anne presses him at every opportunity."

"It is for fear that the child in her belly is a girl." Cromwell knows how these matters work, and sees, quite plainly, what the new queen is up to. "She wants it to rule, no matter what the sex, and that cannot be, if Mary is legitimate. She has not thought it through. Henry's divorce was because his marriage to Katherine was declared invalid. If the marriage is false, then the offspring cannot ascend the throne."

"Then she will win, whatever happens." Rafe sees a bleak future, with Queen Anne outliving Henry, and ruling through her children. It is a dark sounding time, and he wonders how those now falling out of favour will survive.

"No, she will not," Cromwell says. "If she fails to give him a son, Henry will tire of her. He will find another, and throw Anne aside."

"And if she has a boy?"

"Then the king is happy. He has a son, and we will have no need for Queen Anne." Cromwell can see the way ahead, and is beginning to feel better for it. "You recall how we were going to play George Boleyn?"

"I do. You were going to discredit him with

the king, by making him out to be a lover of catamites. Though that might be harder to achieve than we thought."

"How so?"

"He has been swiving Charles Brandon's new mistress, and is on the most intimate terms with several of Anne's ladies." Rafe ponders for a moment. "Though I do believe such men can stand with a foot in each camp. Perhaps, if he was taken, whilst actually…"

"That is not necessary," Thomas Cromwell tells him. "A man can be discredited in many ways. It does not have to be over a woman, or a boy. Is Brandon at court these days?"

"Only when he is tupping George's wife," Rafe replies, sniggering. "Otherwise, he lies low in Suffolk, dodging his numerous creditors."

"Send for him," Cromwell says. "Let Mush deliver the invitation, with a bag of gold to stave off the more urgent claims, and bring him to see me. He shall be my guest at dinner tomorrow night. In fact, I will invite a few old friends. Austin Friars will light up, as in the old days."

"As you wish, master," Rafe says. "Who do you have in mind?"

"We will have Eustace Chapuys round, and ask Uncle Norfolk. He likes a free dinner. Oh, and invite George Boleyn and his father, the magnificent *Monsignour*."

"What?" Rafe Sadler can hardly believe his ears, and thinks Cromwell is indulging in a rare jest. "They hate you."

"They hate everybody," Cromwell says with a huge grin on his face. "How it must stick in

George's throat, every time he sees how well his enemy, Will Draper is doing. We must ask him too, and my dear Miriam. How many is that?"

"Er... let me see... seven, I think." Rafe crosses to the desk, and picks up a quill to make notes. "What about your nephew Richard?"

"Excellent. Then you must come, with your lovely wife to be, dear Ellen Barré, of course." The ageing lawyer claps his hands in pleasure. "Have the cook prepare a feast for twelve. I will find another worthy pair, who will eat at my expense. If he cannot cope, have him ask Mistress Miriam for some help. I hear she willingly caters for rich gentlemen these days."

"Indeed she does," Rafe says, sniffing at the idea of such an extraordinary practice. "Lord's pay her, and she supplies all the food, and the servants for the night. I believe she makes a tidy profit."

"She will make almost fifty thousand this year," Cromwell says. "Who else in England can command such revenue, save the king?"

"Norfolk is worth a hundred thousand."

"Yes, but it is not earned," Cromwell tells him. "I doubt he earns four thousand a year, yet borrows ten from me. Miriam's is revenue. Year on year. She will be the richest woman in England, before she is twenty three."

"Then I hope she hides it well." Rafe has a lawyer's mind, and he resents anything to do with paying taxes, lawful, or not. "Might we not advise her how to use foreign banks?"

"What, and cheat the king's revenue of its fair portion?" Cromwell chuckles. "She pays her taxes, and still makes a fortune. Now, be off, you scoundrelly advocate, and let me make my dinner plans."

*

"Did he eat?" Miriam is just sending off the last boat to market, when her housemaid, Nora, returns. The girl holds up the empty basket for her to see.

"He fair gobbled down your custard, Mistress Miriam," the girl reports, "and he swears he'll eat the rest for his noon meal."

"The man does not look after himself," Miriam Draper mutters. "Still, he has eaten something, and that will have to do. Put the basket back in the kitchen, then come and help me. I must peg out the land for Master Griffiths, and his gang of builders."

Before her untimely death Gwen Draper, Miriam's sister-in-law bought the next plot of riverside land along from Draper's House, and Miriam is set on building another grand house on it. It will be larger, and better built than Draper's House, and she will move into it, once it is finished. As for the old house, she already has a buyer for the property. A rich merchant has offered twice what she paid for it, less than two years before. Her talent for making money is almost beyond belief, and she already counts herself, and her husband, as being amongst the richest folk in London - if not all England.

She has set her pegs, and is explaining her needs to the builder, when the invitation from Austin Friars arrives. She tucks the note into her bodice, and smiles at what it means. Master Thomas is coming out of his black mood. It is almost four months since he lost his precious Lady Agnes, and the hurt must have run deep within him. He will never forget, but the hurt will lessen, with time, she thinks.

"Now, where was I?" she says to Griffiths, the burly master builder.

"Some daft idea about wanting me to put in a cellar," the man grumbles. "It cannot be done."

"Of course it can," Miriam replies, firmly. "You see the pegs? I want your men to dig straight down … ten or twelve feet should suffice."

"Madam… might I draw your attention to the river?" Master Griffiths says, pointing to the fast flowing Thames, less than thirty paces away. "Any hole you dig here, will fill up with water at high tide."

"Then dig it at low tide, and line it with split timbers," she replies. "My husband saw some such thing done in Venice. There, the city sits on a wide lagoon, and is built on stilts."

"More fool them. It will never last."

"It has stood for six hundred years, to date, Master Griffiths," Miriam snaps. "That will be quite long enough for my humble house, thank you!"

"They must have better timbers, or drier water, mistress."

"Dig it out, line it with timber, and tar the seams. Then build a double layer of red brick within," she says. "It will stay dry enough, and I will have my cellars."

"It might work, I suppose." The builder nods

his head. "Though, if it does not…"

"I will fully indemnify you against any failure," Miriam explains. "If you do exactly as I wish, and the water still comes in, I will accept my own stupidity, and still pay you, in full."

"Then I cannot refuse you, Mistress Draper," Griffiths says. "You shall have your cellar … wet or dry, and on time."

"And I want the house to stand alone."

"It will be cheaper to build it up against next door," Griffin says, ringing his hands in exasperation. "That's the usual way."

"Then I must find an *unusual* builder," Miriam snaps. "It will stand alone, with a cellar, and three further floors above. The whole to be built out of god red brick."

"Do you know how much that will cost you?" Griffiths can hardly believe what he hears. "You build a wooden timber frame, and wattle and daub it. You only use bricks at the front, just for show. This is not a cathedral, my girl!"

"Shall I find another builder?"

"There are none as good."

"Then build me what I want."

"My way, it will cost a little under two hundred," he says. "Your way will need clever buttressing, and may cost nearer five hundred."

"I'll have my lawyer draw up a contract," Miriam Draper says, offering her hand. "I use Master Sadler."

"What, not Rafe Sadler?" Griffiths groans inwardly. Sadler is a Thomas Cromwell man, and rubs shoulders with nobility. There will be no room for cutting corners on this job.

"Yes, he is a family friend." Miriam smiles. She knows the price of bricks, and the cost of labour, and knows it can be done for three hundred and fifty. "I will send him four hundred for the job. Three hundred and fifty is for the build, and you will get the other fifty pounds, if you finish before the end of July. Deal?"

"Deal, Mistress Draper… but mark my words … it'll flood!"

*

George Boleyn holds the dinner invitation, as if it were a scorpion. He reads it a second time, then goes in search of his father, who is usually to be found strutting about with the ladies, in the garden. He comes upon him just as the older man is trying to entice Lady Alice Weathers into a leafy arbour.

"Come, my child, let me whisper words of love into that soft, white ear." The old man has stolen words from Tom Wyatt, the current poet of choice, and they seldom fail to woo a lady.

"Father, I must speak with you," George says, his voice full of urgency. "Forgive me Alice, but it is important."

Lady Alice curtseys, and wanders off to find another diversion. Thomas Boleyn is twice her age, after all, and she fancies someone with more life in them. She has heard the rumour that Tom Wyatt the dashing, handsome young poet is back in court, and wonders how to go about meeting him.

"Really, George," *Monsignour* complains. "I

was just about to pick the fruit."

"The lady's tree has been well plucked already, father," George says, petulantly. "They say that Henry is the only man in court who has not tasted that one. I spat out the pips last season!"

"At least she is not as over ripe as your mother," the older Boleyn retorts. "The damned woman refuses to stay down in the country, at one of her brother's castles."

"Uncle Norfolk will not thank you for that," George says. "She has the tongue of a viper, and a temper to match. Now, you must tell me what this is all about." He flourishes the dinner invitation in his father's face.

"Oh, how dreary." *Monsignour* pulls his own from his tunic sleeve. "I thought to be spared your company for one evening. It seems Master Cromwell cannot avoid courting our family. He must be quaking in his boots, now my daughter is queen."

"Thomas Cromwell shivers at nothing, father," George Boleyn replies. "I remember him kicking your arse out of Cardinal Wolsey's chambers, when you tried to wed Anne to that oaf, Harry Percy. I thought he would, as easily, cut your throat."

"You do well to remind me of the incident, my son," Thomas Boleyn sneers. "We will see what his little game is, and cut him back down to size. By the time I have had done with Cromwell, it will be *his* arse that smarts."

"He wants something."

"Then, like the rest, he must pay."

"What if it is something you cannot

bestow?" George asks.

"Dear boy, I am the king's father-in-law. I can do what ever I wish," the older Boleyn says. "Our star is in the ascendancy."

"Then why is Henry so stingy with his gold?" George asks. "He throws titles about well enough, but there is no money to go with them. Nor does he take my advice. I told him that Draper was a rogue, and do you know what he said?"

"No, I fear I missed that one, boy. What did Henry say?"

"He said '*Quite right, George. Go, at once, and force him to draw on you*'. Then, he laughed at me!"

"When Cromwell falls, they all fall," *Monsignour* says. "Colonel Will Draper is no exception. You will be able to live in Austin Friars, and keep your pigs in Draper's House."

"I would rather it were the other way about," George replies, grinning. "For Draper keeps a very pretty wife, and I would be glad to draw my dagger on her!"

"Draper is away a great deal," *Monsignour* replies. "Why can you not call on the girl then, and press home the advantage? By the time the fellow returns, she will be broken to the saddle, and we might all have a ride."

"She was attacked in her home, about a year ago," George says. "She drew a dagger, and slew the fellow on her stairs, or so the story runs. I have no wish to be skewered, whilst struggling to get out of my hose. No, father, I will bide my time."

2   Spring

The smell of wet grass, on a fine Spring morning, is a memory that reminds Will Draper of his time fighting in Ireland. It, along with the constant buzzing of insects, and the awkward gambolling of the new born lambs in the meadows, makes him feel as alive as can be.

"A very good morning to you, sir." The man doffs his cap, and bows low. Will still has a problem with his new status as the King's Examiner, and returns the bow awkwardly. "Have I the pleasure of addressing Colonel Will Draper, the King's Examiner?"

"You do, sir, and you are…?"

"Marmaduke, sir," he replies. "Walter Marmaduke, head steward of Oxton Manor. The house is less than a mile ahead."

"Then let us get on, Master Marmaduke," Will tells him, "for I doubt the body will last long, even in this mild heat. This is the second day, is it not?"

"We sent right away, sir," the steward says, fearful of attracting blame to himself. "I found her, you see. It fair shook me, and I knew the magistrate would blame me for any delay."

"How come you to know of my office?" Will is glad of an adventure, but cannot help wonder how the steward of a small estate in Suffolk is so aware.

"Master Charles, your honour," Marmaduke explains. "Sir Anthony Clough is one of his tenants, and he was here just after Christmas. His lordship told a fine tale of how you investigate matters that affect the king."

"You mean the Duke of Suffolk?" Will nods to himself. Brandon has spread his fame, without making it clear that he is meant only to investigate matters that involve the crown. "I fear he misled you, as this does not touch upon the king."

"Beggin' your pardon, sir, but it does," the old steward replies. "Lady Clough … that is the deceased …did often entertain King Hal, when he was still but a prince. There was some talk of a love match, but she wed another, and then, Sir Anthony ended up with her. I reckon Henry will want to know how his old love died, do not you, sir?"

Will reckons that Henry does not remember the woman from twenty years, or more, back, and guesses that there has been a hundred such ladies in his life since then. Still, it is a pleasant day, and there is the chance of resolving a mystery.

"You say you found the woman?"

"I did. I was going to saddle up the master's favourite hunter, and there she was … hanging there. I was out of that barn in a moment, and barred the door. Then I sent a fast rider, with orders to find you."

"He did well," Will says, recalling the annoyance with which Miriam had thrown open the bedroom window at three in the morning. "My wife took pity on the poor exhausted boy, and found him a warm place in the kitchen. He will be following on, no doubt, having been fed, almost to death by her."

"My lad, sir," Marmaduke explains. "He is the only one I trust. I put a man on guard, and set off to meet you. I am amazed at the speed of your coming, Colonel Draper."

"I set off at first light, and have been on the road these last four hours. Though you might have been better advised sending your lad to Ipswich, Norwich, King's Lynn, or even Boston." Will reins Moll in, and stares down at the manor. It is a big, modern red brick affair, with a moat, a small gatehouse, and a church, close by. The surrounding gardens are immaculate. Some fifty yards to the rear of the main house is a large, wooden barn.

"None of those places, though so full of people, have any real law, sir. This is not for a mere Sheriff." Will does not argue. Country folk are a constant mystery to him.

"Apart from cutting her down," he says, "did you disturb anything else, my friend?"

"Cut her down?" the steward looks aghast. "Not I, sir. You must not touch a suicide, for fear of the evil spirit within, a-comin' without!"

"Ah, quite, I see your point." Will has little truck with the supernatural, and does not believe evil spirits inhabit the bodies of dead men. Were that to be the case, he would be overrun with malevolent spirits from all those whose lives he had taken. "Still, someone must do it."

"You *are* the King's Examiner, Colonel Draper."

"Yes, I am," Will says, smiling cheerfully. Riding for hours, and cutting down hanging corpses for a hundred pounds a year, when his wife is making almost a thousand pounds a week from selling cheese, fish oil, nails, salt, spices and wool, suddenly seems a strange way to earn a living. "Will you at least stand by the door, with a dagger?"

"A dagger?" Marmaduke looks horrified. "Whatever for, sir?"

"If there is any evil spirit in there, stab the second thing to come out of the barn... for the first will be me!"

"It takes a brave man to jest so," the steward mutters.

"Then let us hear no more about ghouls and spirits, fellow," Will tells him. "Have a carpenter prepare a suitable box, and warn the gravedigger that he must have a plot dug before noon. The lady will be ready for the ground, and no mistake."

"The priest will not let her rest in hallowed ground."

"What?"

"She hanged herself, sir."

"Is that not for me to find out?" Will shakes his head in disbelief. "Is the priest a Roman, or of the new church?"

"New, sir. The old priest was harmless enough, but would not stop chunnering away in Latin, so some soldiers knocked him on the head, and dragged him off to Ipswich gaol. The new man is much better. He says there is no purgatory, sir, and that God speaks directly to King Harry, not to the Pope... I mean ... the Bishop of Rome. Is that right?"

"I know not," Will says. "What does the new English bible say on the matter?"

"I do not know, sir. My reading is not that good. The new man says that Jesus washed away all of man's sins, and that we will all go straight up up to heaven. He says that in our father's house there are many mansions."

"Good for him. I doubt he will begrudge a poor woman one small piece of ground then." Will slips from Moll's back, and is disturbed by the sound of horses in distress. He glances over at the steward, who shrugs.

"I dared not go in," he explains. "They'll be ready for watering and feeding by now."

"God's teeth, man!" Will unbars the barn door, and steps inside. The bright morning sun illuminates the interior, and he gasps in horror. A woman, of middle years, is hanging from a crossbeam, with a toppled milking stool at her feet, and a sad, bloated look on her face. Worse of all is the smell. A cloud of flies attest to the start of the rotting process. "Get the horses out, and see to them."

"But, sir…I,"

"Now, or I will put my boot up your arse, fellow!" Will is gratified when the threat works, and the steward crosses to the stalls, where two mares are kept. The King's Examiner approaches the hanging body, and stares. He has seen many hangings in his time, but never that of a woman. Her dress is of a fine make, and she is obviously of good birth. "This is definitely your mistress, Lady Clough?"

"No doubt," Marmaduke replies, tremulously. He even crosses himself for good measure. "Lady Isabella Clough."

"And her husband?"

"Mad with grief," the steward replies, shooing the two mares outside. "He's in the big house, with one of the lads keeping an eye on him."

"That is for the best," Will says softly. He circles the body, which is now twisting in the slight breeze from the door. At length, he stoops, and stands the stool back up on its legs. "Such a terrible way to die. I am going to cut your lady down now, Master Marmaduke. Can you help, or must you look away?"

The steward takes a deep breath. It is the bravest thing he has ever been asked to do, and his poor soul is scarcely up to it, but he nods his head, and comes forward. He takes the body around the knees, closes his eyes, and waits until Will Draper climbs onto the stool, and slices through the rope.

"Arghh!" Marmaduke staggers, and might easily fall, if Will does not jump down, and help take the weight. "Sweet Jesus, but the smell!"

"Lower her down, my friend There, that will do," Will pats the fellow on the shoulder. "Bravely done. Now, leave me to my task, and find that priest."

"With pleasure, Colonel Draper," Marmaduke replies. He scuttles away, gulping in huge breaths of fresh air, and wiping away tears. He has known Lady Isabella for almost twenty years, and cannot believe she is gone.

Will examines the length of rope, and sees that it is not unlike the good quality three strand jute his wife buys in, from the rope makers, in Castleton. The Derbyshire village, dominated by a derelict Norman castle, survives on its plaiting skills. It is strong, and supple enough to fashion a noose with.

He sits down on the stool then, and contemplates the cold, dead eyes of the hanged woman. They are milking over, and the pallid skin is assuming a more marbled effect, with every passing moment. There is a small, nagging thought at the back of his mind, and he worries at it, until the answer comes.

Of course, he thinks. There has to be a stool, how else did she gain enough height for the final drop? Then again, why choose a barn to kill yourself in? What if one of the farm labourers had happened by, or the steward had come looking earlier?

He wonders what it is that drives someone to so desperate an act, and kneels beside the body. It is a distasteful task, but Will Draper grips the noose, and loosens it from her neck. The head lolls, making him jump back in alarm. He scolds himself for his stupidity, and resumes his examination. The mark left by the heavy rope is a livid purple, and, here and there, the skin is broken, and crusted with flecks of dried blood.

"Damn," he says, softly to himself. "Why could they not have just called for the local Sheriff?" He turns the lady onto her side, and examines how she is dressed. After a moment, he smiles, and shakes his head. "Now then," he says, "what have we here?"

*

Walter Marmaduke is not having a good day. Having had to help cut down a suicide, he is now trying to explain matters to Father Matthew Brady, who is preparing for a church service.

"But father, you must come," he says, "for the King's Examiner demands…"

"Demands?" Matthew Brady glowers at the old servant. "I am a man of God, Master Marmaduke, and none commands me, save Himself … or his representative, King Henry. Nor must you call me 'father'. I am a reverend gentleman, not your blasted father. If I have to read the bible from end to end, every Sunday, I will beat the way of things into you peasants!"

"That is not necessary, fath… I mean Reverend," Marmaduke stammers. "I believe there is no purgatory, and I believe that the Bishop of Rome does not speak to God. I spurn Latin, and have faith in the new English writings. I also know Jesus is my saviour, but there is a man, in my master's top barn, with a dead body, and he bids me bring you to him."

"Cannot you bring the dead body here?" Brady asks.

"He will not move it yet, as he is investigating it."

"Dear Christ! What kind of rogue is it that wishes to investigate the dead? Is he some sort of…"

"No, Reverend, you misunderstand. The manner of her death is … unusual, and he would have you come, and reassure him that you will bury her."

"Ah, a suicide." Brady scratches his beard, and places a wide brimmed black hat on his head. "I'll say a few words over the poor creature, and bury her up by the church wall. That way, she may climb over on Judgement Day, and seek salvation. Come on."

*

"We should serve up a lot of pork," Miriam says, as she peruses Thomas Cromwell's provisional menu. "Seeing as how the Boleyns are coming, and they are akin to pigs."

"Hush, my girl," Cromwell says, from his desk. He has his godson, Gwyllam dangling on one knee. "I want it to be a night to remember. I want nothing, but the best, and I want you to supervise it for me. You must charge me, as you charge your great lords."

"I cannot do that," Miriam admits, "for my conscience will not let me. If I charge you at but half my usual rate, I will still make too fine a profit. I charge each to their worth, you see."

"You overcharge the Duke of Norfolk, and Warwick?" Cromwell smiles, and nods his approval. "How could I not be your father? You and I are so alike."

"You are my father, sir… or as close as any can be," she says. "Gwyllam's first word shall be 'grandpa', I wager."

"Your respect, and love, is worth more than any amount of gold to me, Miriam," he replies. "Has Will fully forgiven me yet?"

"He holds you above all men," Miriam says, truthfully. "What about custard tarts? After all this meat, they will want something to lighten the palate."

"I am in your hands." Cromwell considers

for a moment. "I ask only that you do not poison those you do not like."

"That is more the queen's style," Miriam tells the Privy Councillor. "I swear, that woman is so unpopular. Did you know that the people shout at her in the street, and the other night, someone daubed *'Whore of Babylon'* on the north wall of Whitehall Palace?"

"Goodness. In English, or Latin?" Cromwell cannot help but smile at the idea of one of his agents writing *'Babylon meretrix'* in foot high letters on a wall. He pays a fine young rogue, named Digby Waller, to cause these small discomforts to Queen Anne, and employs him to do those small tasks that are now below his nephew Richard, or even Mush Draper.

"It is a Tyndale man," Miriam says. "Will is commissioned by the king to find the perpetrators, but has had little luck so far. It is not like him to struggle with a solution. He sets men to watch, and uses your own agents to mix in with the crowds, but all to no avail."

"Poor Will, I fear he must fail."

"Oh, no, I doubt it," Miriam says, giving Cromwell a knowing look. "He already knows enough to describe the felon. He is a head taller than I, is well educated, and is left handed. He also has a crack in the sole of his right boot."

"And how does he come to these conclusions?" Cromwell asks. He is stunned at the truth of these deductions, and marvels at how proficient his old agent is becoming.

"From the height of the letters above the ground," Miriam explains. "When you are painting, you stand so... and raise your arm so. The letter height means his head is about a foot lower, hence he is a head taller than me. The painted letters all start, and finish, with the brush being pressed on, and then slid off. The strokes are those made by a left handed man."

"And the boot?" Cromwell has actually noticed the crack in Waller's boot, and remarked that he should treat himself to a better pair.

"He has stood in mud once. The imprint is quite clear," Miriam tells her benefactor. "He should buy a new pair at once. It would be a shame to hang, all for a worn sole, would it not, Master Tom?"

"Perhaps the silly game might cease," Cromwell says. "In that way, Will shall be seen to have stopped it, and so much improve his standing with Henry."

"I'd rather it were the queen who loved him more," the young Jewess complains. "For Henry hangs on her every word. Let me take this list away, and I will ensure your guests have a wonderful feast. Shall I supply the wine... for my stocks are better than yours."

"You excel in so many ways, my dear girl," Cromwell says. It is time to relinquish his hold on little Gwyllam, and he is pleased when the child cries, on being handed back to his mother.

"See, he loves you already," Miriam says. "Might I misuse your love for my family to suggest something, Master Tom?"

"Go on." Cromwell cannot think of anything he might refuse the girl.

"The guest list is unbalanced," Miriam says.

"Might it not be better if more ladies were invited?"

"Ah, I see." Cromwell shakes his head, sadly. It is too soon since his sad loss, and Lady Agnes is still in his heart. "Who did you have in mind?"

"Bernice Goossens," Miriam says. "She is a widow. Her husband used to handle my Flemish cloth trade for me. He died a month ago. She is a goodly woman, and a fine housekeeper. She is in London settling her late husband's affairs."

"Is she pretty?"

"Does that matter in a wife?"

"True. Can she speak English?"

"English, Flemish, French, and Latin," Miriam tells him.

"A veritable Plato," Thomas Cromwell mutters. "There are many better men in London, my dear. Invite her if you must, but I am not ready to meet another woman just yet."

"Perhaps she might catch the eye of one of the other guests," Miriam says, straight faced. She knows Cromwell is ready to have another woman in his life. He needs female influence in his world, and if he marries a young enough widow, he might yet have more children. His son, Gregory is always away in Oxford, and is more his mother's son, than his father's.

The boy loves adventure, racing greyhounds, riding to hounds, and all the other gentlemanly pursuits. He will never be able to step into his father's shoes, and if Austin Friars is to survive, there must be a worthy successor, and soon.

"I would not wish her to marry Norfolk,"

Tom Cromwell says. "For the misery would be too much for her. We will find her a good man, Miriam… I promise!"

*

Will is crouching over the body, when he senses that someone is behind him. He slips one hand to the throwing knife in his boot, and turns. Framed in the light of the open door, is a large, black shape. The figure steps forward, and touches his fingers to the brim of his wide black hat.

"Colonel Draper?" The figure moves closer, and resolves itself into that of a big, well muscled man in his late twenties. He is wearing a long black coat, and a wide hat. Around his neck, he has a white kerchief tied. "I am the Reverend Brady. You sent for me, I believe?"

"This lady is above ground over long, sir," Will says, as he stands to his feet. "Would you refuse her your ministrations?"

"I am not a papist, Colonel Draper," Brady replies. "Nor do I demand silver before I utter the words of Our Lord Jesus Christ, Son of God, and Redeemer of Mankind."

"Amen," Will says. "You are a Tyndale man then?"

"I am a Christian, sir," Brady replies. "I believe Englishmen should hear the Holy Bible, in their native tongue. If that makes me a Tyndale man, then so be it." He crosses to the body, and prays. After a moment he wipes his eyes, and turns away. "Forgive me, sir, but I knew this lady well, and never a kinder woman lived. Now there will be none to stay her husband's hand."

"Sir Anthony Clough?" Will senses that Brady dislikes the man, and probes further. "Was it an unhappy marriage?"

"Do you mean, did he drive her to kill herself?" the reverend asks.

"No, I do not," Will responds. "I mean, were they happy? Did they quarrel? Was he ever brutal to her?"

"I see. I have only been in charge of the church for a short time, but I farmed close by, for several years. Lady Isabella was married to Sir Arthur Destry, and it was a happy union, though childless. Sir Arthur died about five years ago, leaving Lady Isabella with a decent fortune, and a lot of land. The land was deeded from the Duke of Suffolk, who did not want a widow as his tenant, so he insisted she re-marry. His choice was Sir Anthony Clough, a penniless, card playing, friend. He was ten years my lady's junior, and was soon whoring about King's Lynn, and Boston, spending her wealth."

"It was his right, once they were wed," Will says. It is a hard world for women, he thinks, and muses at how Miriam must feel, knowing that everything she will ever earn is his, by law. He would never abuse the situation, but he is the exception that proves the rule. Most husbands simply take everything, as a right. "So, they argued?"

"They did." Reverend Brady kneels, and closes the dead woman's eyes. They spring back open, making him jump back in horror.

"It is the stiffness," Will explains. "I know

not why, but the dead grow stiff. I have seen those killed in battle, a few days later, and they grow softer again, just before they start to really rot. That is when you will be able to close her eyes. Or you might put a couple of coins on the lids to hold them down."

"I have no coins," Brady says. "The Lord commands that I give all I have to the needy."

"Here, take these coppers," Will says. "Give them to the poor, when you are done."

"Thank you." The man closes the eyes again, and balances a coin on each lid. "Ah, it works. How came she to this, Colonel Draper? Lady Isabella was the strongest woman I have ever known. She stood up to Sir Anthony, and found ways to hide her wealth."

"I wager that drove him mad with anger."

"Sir, your questions disturb me," Brady says. "Pray tell me what is on your mind."

"Come, and let me show you what I have discovered," Will says. "Then I ask that you accompany me to the house, where Sir Anthony is 'mad with grief'.

*

"When this is over, I shall horsewhip you, Marmaduke," Sir Anthony snarls. "Then I will turn you, and your family out of their cottages, and burn them down. You will starve, like stray dogs, and I will laugh. What say you to that?"

"I cannot unbar your door, sir," Marmaduke calls back through the wooden barrier. "Her Ladyship is dead, and you must be here to answer whatever questions there are."

"It is almost two days," Clough shouts back. "How long does it take to get a Sheriff? By Christ's bollocks, but I shall have the woman in the ground, and any law sent packing!"

"Colonel Draper is the King's Examiner," Marmaduke replies. "He comes from London, and will get to the reason Lady Isabella hanged herself. Why, you dog… sir … it was you and your whoring, and gambling, that drove her to it."

"And what of it?" Sir Anthony cries. "It is all mine, to do with as I please, you idiot! This King's Examiner will know his law, and release me. Then, by God, you will all feel my wrath!"

"Unbar the door, please." Will Draper and the Reverend Brady fill the passage behind the steward. "We will have words with Sir Anthony."

"About time," Sir Anthony says. "I have not had a drink for two days, save watered wine with the meals they brought me. Can you believe it, sirs, two days, kept from my business."

"Sir, your wife is dead," Brady says.

"By her own hand," Sir Anthony Clough says, harshly. "It was coming. I saw how unhappy she was, but what can a young fellow do with these older women? I should never have taken her on … though the fortune always comes in damned handy. Get her buried, priest, and be damned to her. I have things to do."

"You have a black heart, sir," Brady says. "God is all about us, and sees the wickedness that men do. Beware, lest you destroy your immortal soul."

"Oh, bugger off!" Clough waves his arms as

if shooing away an insect. "And as for you, Master Examiner, what brings you here?"

"I come to examine your wife's death, sir," Will says. "I see that one of the bed drapes is missing."

"What?" Sir Anthony frowns. "Being washed, I suppose. It might have been soiled, or in need of mending."

"Or stained by the grass," Will says. "Whatever the reason, it is off, and with the washerwoman."

"No doubt."

"Master Marmaduke, who actually is Lady Isabella's washer woman?" Will asks the steward.

"Why, my wife, sir." Marmaduke replies, somewhat mystified. "She tends to all the linen, and keeps the wall hangings, and bed drapes, in good condition. It is her duty."

"Has she washed today?"

"No, sir. I think the shock of it has quite unnerved her. The washing has been left these last two days."

"Then I shall need to see it."

"As you wish, sir." Marmaduke scurries away.

"As you wish? You dribbling piece of piss, it is for me to say what happens here," Clough snarls. "Now, I suggest you all piss off, out of *my* house!"

"It is yours because you married Lady Isabella," Will says.

"What of it?"

"You married, thinking to use the poor woman's fortune for your own ends, but Lady

Isabella was too shrewd for you."

"What, a woman?" Clough grins. "She was not so clever after a few slaps. A good whipping settles them down, Colonel Draper. I wager you know who runs your household."

"I do sir," Will replies, coldly. "Lady Isabella arranged to hide most of her wealth, and was using it to better the lot of her tenants. You found out, two nights ago, and flew into a rage. The servants could hear you cursing and swearing, but she bested you. You could see no other way of getting her wealth, so you came up with a clever plan."

"I told her that she was a barren old sow, and that no gentleman would ever look at her again." Sir Anthony smiles at the recollection. "She slapped my face, and walked out on me. I thought she was in another bedroom, sulking. Had I known she was going to kill herself, I would have had the servants stop her. I mean, suicide is a crime, after all is said and done. I would have had her locked away, as the mad woman she was."

"One bed hanging, sir," Marmaduke presents the heavy, embroidered bed drape, and Reverend Brady takes it and holds it up for all to see. "The wife says she will never get those stains out."

"Why it looks as though it has been dragged across a damp field," Will says. "And the tie?" Marmaduke holds up the thin, braided cord that is used to hold the drapes back. "Ah, as I thought, gentlemen. Reverend Brady, I beg of you, examine the cord. Do you see anything on it?"

"I do. Brown flecks of ... blood, is it?"

"This is preposterous!" Clough tries to leave the room, but his way is barred. "What are you saying? The woman hanged herself. You *must* have seen that for yourself?"

"I saw exactly what you wanted Marmaduke to see." Will takes the cord in each fist, and taughtens it. "You thought he would cut her down, and send for you. A quick burial, and that would be that. Unfortunately, your steward loved his mistress, and felt her death should be looked at, if only to show you up for the swine you are."

"You miserable dog, I shall call you out for that," Clough says. "I challenge you, sir. Either retract what you say, or I *demand* satisfaction!"

"What I saw was a remarkable woman who managed to tie a heavy rope to a beam, above her reach … even using a stool. Then I saw that, when she was hanging, that same stool was too low for her to stand on. Lady Isabella would have to have been about your height, Sir Anthony."

"Pistol, or sword, you cur," Clough snarls. "I will satisfy my honour, as the law allows, then deal with these servants, as I see fit."

"You lost your argument, insulted the lady, and received an embarrassing slap for your trouble," Will continues. "Being a coward, you waited for her to sleep, then took the cord, and strangled her. A clear case of murder. Your servants would have taken you up, and called for the Sheriff. The end result would have been your own hanging."

"That is a lie!"

"So, you wrapped her in the drape, and dragged her to the barn. There, you fashioned a noose, and strung her body up. I found two distinct rope marks. A wider bruise, hiding a narrower one, which cut into her neck. I have two witnesses, who will swear to my conclusions, and my report will state that you murdered Lady Isabella Clough."

"I am a friend of Charles Brandon, Duke of Suffolk, Master Examiner," Clough says, and he smiles at the power this gives him. "It is for him to decide my fate, and he will readily take my word for it … that the old sow hanged herself."

"I dare say he will, sir," Will says, and nods his agreement. "Now, there is the other matter; the business of you insulting the king."

"How so, sir?" Clough feels he is on safe ground. He knows Brandon is fool enough to take his word. "I simply called you 'a dog' as I recall."

"And called me out. I offered the first insult, as I recall," Will says. "Is that so, Reverend Brady?"

"You called him a swine," the man of God confirms. "Though later, you did call him a coward. I fear you must retract what you said, sir, or defend your honour."

"I am the King's Examiner, sir, I cannot retract, lest it besmirches my honour, and reflects on his." Will drops the cord, and bows to a startled Clough. "Pistol or sword, *you filthy cur*."

"You mean it?" Sir Anthony Clough looks from one man to the other, and sees that it is meant in earnest. "Marmaduke, fetch my pistol case. The silver handled pair given to me by the Duke of Suffolk. Oh, and the heavy sabre, from the great hall. I see you already have yours, sir."

"A German blade," Will says, touching the hilt. He has lost count of the times he has told the tale of how he took it from the hand of a defeated

Irish chieftain, or of how many men he has killed with it. "Shall we step outside, sir?"

"If I kill you, the murder charge will die with you, will it not?"

"Ah, you wish it to be to the death?" Will Draper nods his agreement. They step out into the fresh Spring morning, and move away from the house. A dozen indoor servants and some farm workers are dotted about, wondering what is to befall them, now their mistress is dead.

Walter Marmaduke comes from the house, carrying a wooden box, and a sword, free of its scabbard. He thrusts the point of the sword into the soft grass, and the soil beneath, and opens the beautifully decorated box. Will draws his own blade and sticks it likewise into the ground, about twenty paces apart from Sir Anthony's. It is to the death. They will use pistols, and resort to their blades, if both miss.

"Choose," Sir Anthony says. He is an expert shot, and is sure he can put his ball into Will Draper at ten paces. Unfortunately, his opponent might still have time to fire, and inflict a serious wound. It is time to take precautions. Will Draper picks one of the beautiful duelling pistols up, nods to his foe, and starts to pace off ten steps.

"Dog!" Clough snarls, even as he raises his pistol, and from a range of seven or eight paces, discharges it into Will Draper's exposed back. The flash, and sharp crack makes the witnesses blink, or turn away. Only Will Draper remains unmoved. Slowly, he turns to face a horrified Clough. At this range, the lead ball should have punched a hole through the man's spine.

"Dear me," Walter Marmaduke says, opening his palm, to show two lead rounds. "I forgot to put these in."

Will Draper cannot believe how stupid he has been, to turn his back on a man, whom he has already condemned as a wife murderer. He raises his own pistol, and fires. The spurt of flame, and belch of acrid smoke billows out, to no effect.

Sir Anthony Clough still flinches, then curses, and runs for his sword, where it is stabbed into the soft soil. It is a heavy weapon, designed to cleave through armour, and takes a lot of strength to wield it. He advances on Will Draper, who pulls free his own blade.

"This sword was made in Germany, by the best forge masters in the world," he says, as he moves closer to Clough. "It is folded and folded, until the steel is stronger than any other."

Clough launches a sudden attack, and swings the big sabre, like an axe, at Will's head. He dances back a pace, and draws a dagger with his left hand. It will act as a useful parry if he is too slow to get out of the way. He sets himself for the next attack, and smiles, like a fox.

"Now, where was I?" Will ponders. "Oh, yes. The hilt is made from a tongue of the same steel, sheathed with hardwood, riveted through with iron fastenings, and finally, bound with a leather cord, soaked in vinegar. Good try!" Will jumps aside, and avoids a second, lethal blow. "The vinegar shrinks the leather, making it fast, and it provides a wonderful grip. Of course, the main advantage of my sword, is that it is lighter than yours, and can be used one handed. See?"

Sir Anthony Clough cannot believe what has happened. As he makes his third lunge, Will Draper manages to flick aside the point of his heavy blade, step inside the swing, and drive his dagger home, with lethal effect. The thin blade goes in, under the rib, as Mush has often demonstrated, and punctures the heart.

The wife murderer blinks once, then shudders, and falls to his knees. The King's Examiner stoops with him, until the light of life goes from his eyes. Then he eases his body onto its back, and withdraws the knife. There is a small fountain of blood, and it is over.

"Fairly done, sir?" Will asks of Brady, and the Reverend Gentleman solemnly nods his head.

"He called you out, and he lost," Brady says to him. "I will also swear to his guilt in the matter of his wife's death. She shall be buried in the church, and her dog of a husband can go in a hole near the lych gate. It will stop his wicked spirit from wandering."

"Now we have no master," Walter says.

"You saved my life, Master Marmaduke," Will says. "I should have known he would try to play me false."

"I knew how he thought," Marmaduke replies. "I dared not arm the pistols, and hoped you could use a sword. Thank God you can, sir!"

"I will call on Charles Brandon," Will Draper says. "He owes me, and we are close to being friends. I will have him lease the estate to my wife."

"Your wife, sir?"

"It is a long tale," Will says. "You will find

her a benign mistress, as long as you play fair by her. The church will prosper, and she will see everyone benefits."

"Amen to that," Reverend Brady says. "By God, but this business has given me a thirst. Will you take some ale with me, Colonel Draper, and you too, Walter?"

"I must decline," Will Draper says. "I promised my wife a day or two of my company, and must return home, as fast as Moll can carry me."

"Then God bless you, Colonel Draper," the Reverend Brady replies. "May he grant you both the few days rest you so crave."

3 New Faces

"*Denna stad luktar illa!*" The tall, thin man stokes his beard as he pronounces his view of London. His companion, laden with bags, simply scowls Of course London smells badly, he thinks, it is like any other city they have visited. Cities are made of people, and people stink. He beckons a small boy over, who is standing on the dockside, where he waits for the chance to earn a few coppers from new arrivals.

"Your service, master," the boy says, bowing to the strangely dressed duo. "What can I do for you?"

"Lodgings," the shorter, fatter, younger one says, in a voice that is not used to speaking English. "We wish good rooms. My master is Aldo Mercurius, Master of Alchemy to the court of Prince Ygor of Lithuania. He comes to see your king. Once we are settled in, you will go tell your king, that we here! Yes?"

"Gor' but Old Hal will love you," the boy mutters. "Come on then. Here, sir, I'll take that bag."

"No!" The tall alchemist snatches the battered old bag, and clutches it to his narrow chest. "For your own sake. I keep safe. Yes?"

"Please yourself," The boy decides that the Fighting Cock might be too lively for the two strangers, and decides to take them to the Elephant instead. It is still rough, but the rooms are clean, and the girls are usually pox free, and not too expensive. They set off, on foot, and soon have a small, but very curious, crowd following them.

London is full of time wasters, with nothing to do, except create their own fun. There are thousands who live off their masters: Lords who dole out free bread, and the odd coppers, because they see power in numbers. It is a false vision, of course, as most will back anyone who is stupid enough to support their lazy ways. One scoundrel decides to lead the way, and declares the coming of strangers in a loud voice.

"Make way... make way for the Royal Alchemist," he shouts. "Lest he do magic you unto death!"

"Go on, do some magic," another calls, and the crowd laughs. Master Mercurius keeps a dignified silence, until they reach the door of the selected inn. There, he turns to the crowd, and raises his hands for silence. His assistant kneels at his feet, with his hands crossed over his chest.

"Behold, unbelievers," the younger man shouts. "See the power of Aldo Mercurius!" There is a sudden flash of light, and a cloud of acrid smoke. A woman in the crowd screams, and grown men fall back in horror. The alchemist has vanished, leaving behind the pungent smell of The Devil. His assistant stands, bows to the astonished crowd, and closes the door in their faces.

The secret ways of the sect of the alchemists have come to London, and its greatest practitioner is amongst them. Word will travel far and wide, and by nightfall, all of the city will know that a sorcerer walks amongst them. Doors will be locked, and charms hung above windowpanes, against the evil eye.

The boy pockets the silver coin, given to him

by the foreign gentleman, and sets off whistling to himself. It is his duty to report anything unusual back to Austin Friars, and there is nothing more unusual than a couple of real magicians lodging at the Elephant and Castle.

With luck, Master Rafe, or even Cromwell himself will give him a further reward. He works his way through the densely crowded streets, just back from the river, and finally makes it to Austin Friars. There is a high wall running all about the property, but the main gate is never closed. The lad nods to another boy, who often acts as gatekeeper.

"Any one of them in, Dick?" he asks.

"Master Cromwell," the second boy says. "He's been waiting for you, Alfie."

"For me?" the lad is surprised, and wonders if he is in some kind of trouble.

"You've been down near the ships, ain't you?"

"Yes." Alfie is relieved, for Thomas Cromwell wants only whomsoever has dock duty that day.

"Then you are to go straight on in." Dick resumes his place on the low stool, and returns to watching all who pass by.

The boy shrugs. There is always something going on around Austin Friars, so he should not be surprised when the master knows things before they even happen. He slips through the open front door, and hovers outside the door to the master's study. Only once has he ever been inside the book lined room, and the smell of leather, and the incalculable value of the precious books leaves him awestruck.

"Come in, child," Cromwell calls. "No need to loiter."

"Beg pardon, master, but I just…"

"Came from the wharf."

"Saints preserve my soul, guv'nor," the lad whispers. "Have you got watchers watchin' us watchers now?"

"Never mind that," Thomas Cromwell says, smiling at the child's confusion. "Where did you lodge them?"

"The Elephant, sir."

"A wise choice."

"One of them said he was an alchemist, and then he alchemised himself to nothing," the boy says. "A puff of smoke, and he was gone. It fair stank of Old Hob, an' no mistake!"

"Ah, a true magician," Thomas Cromwell says. "Here, take this letter to them. Tell them that I set the finest table in England, and that both are welcome, this evening. Warn them that the streets are dangerous after dark, and I will send some of my young men to escort them."

"Yes, sir," the lad says, staring at the letter in his hand. "Forgive me, master, but I am a stupid sort, and must ask this of you. How can you write a letter to a man who is not there yet?"

"I saw it all, in my magic crystal ball," Tom Cromwell tells the wide eyed lad without cracking a smile. He takes a silver coin from his purse, and holds it out. The boy goes to take it, and it is, of a sudden, not there. Tom Cromwell opens his other hand, and shows off the very same silver coin. "There, that is Master Cromwell's Magickery, my dear boy. Now… be off, and deliver that letter to to these strangers who come amongst us!"

*

"You should not waste your power like that," the short man says to the alchemist. "These people are as easy to please as little children."

"Dangerous children, Popo," Aldo Mercurius says. "They cheer one day, and want to burn you the next. It is good that they fear us a little."

"Shall I have the inn keeper prepare us some food?"

"No." Mercurius touches fingertips to his head, and strokes his long, pointed beard with the other hand. "There is a dinner invitation already coming to us. Tonight, we will dine with the greatest in the land."

"Will we have to impress them?" Popo asks. The alchemist smiles, and shakes his head.

"There is no point in trying to impress Thomas Cromwell," he says. "There is not a sharper mind in all Europe."

"What about Erasmus?"

"That old fool?" the alchemist sneers. "You bring his name up, merely to annoy me, Popo. He spends his days talking to God, and his nights writing down His replies. Can he make himself vanish, levitate a table, or bring a black cat from an empty box?"

"He does not have to roam the world," Popo mumbles.

"Master Thomas Cromwell is very clever," Mercurius says, and taps a finger to the side of his nose. "He lives by the basest trickery, yet understands the innate truth behind the magic and mystery of alchemy."

"Then he is the second cleverest man in the world, after you?" Popo says, grinning. The alchemist considers the question for a moment, then shakes his head.

"There was another, but he is dead."

"Ah, the great Machiavelli," the alchemist's assistant says, and starts rummaging through their luggage. It is his place to ensure every scrap of sulphur, each piece of equipment, and all the necessary ingredients are to hand, and he never fails to please.

"Machiavelli was a genius," Mercurius says. "He said *'it would be best to be both loved, and feared. But since the two rarely come together, anyone compelled to choose will find greater security in being feared, rather than being loved.* It is a maxim that I have taken to heart, my little friend."

"Which gown shall you wear?"

"The silken black, with the symbols on it," Aldo replies. "Oh, and the black cap. The one that flops over my ears. If Cromwell wants a demonstration of my powers, then let it be so."

"Please, master ... do not frighten them too much. Remember what happened in Paris."

"Ah, yes. Fear can make men behave in the most unfortunate of ways," the alchemist says, as he recalls a hurried flight in the night, from a howling mob. "Perhaps Machiavelli was not quite right. Perhaps there must be a little love mixed in with the fear."

"These English favour the rack, and the

stake," Popo advises.

"Not Cromwell. I hear he is a most gentle soul... when it suits his purpose."

"They do say he sets a fine table," says Popo. "It will be a change from the terrible ship's food!"

*

By an odd coincidence Thomas Cromwell has, at that very moment, a book laid open before him. It is 'The Prince' and details how a political mind works to gain its own ends. Cromwell is saddened to read that, a constant of much of Machiavelli's work, is that the ruler must adopt the most unsavoury policies, for the sake of the continuance of his regime.

This is not something he wishes to happen in England, during Henry's rule. With the right sort of direction, he is sure that the king's reign can be largely benevolent. Unfortunately, there are those who would ruin his carefully laid plans, and he is forced to take remedial action.

Next to the Italian book is another. It is his infamous black leather bound '*Vindicatio*'. The book is whispered about, amongst those in the know, and it contains details of all those who have crossed Thomas Cromwell in the past. It contains many names, and a good part of them have been crossed through, as they have been claimed by death, or ruined.

Sir Thomas More's name adorns one page, but Cromwell has no wish to destroy the man any further. It is enough that he has lost his place, and is a broken old man, living out his last years in his Chelsea estate… Utopia.

There are four pages, dedicated to the Boleyn family, and these entries are amongst the most recent of all. Until her marriage, Anne was little more than an irritant, but now, he sees, her family have become the greatest threat. *Monsignour*, and his son, George, are taking an active role in opposition, and must be challenged, before they grow too powerful.

Thomas Cromwell sighs. Then he picks up a freshly penned quill, dips it into his ink pot, and begins to make notes. That very evening he must entertain two of his worst enemies, and reassure them that, though in different camps, he means them no ill will. For their part, they will pretend friendship, and look for some weakness, whereby they can tear down Austin Friars, and condemn him to failure… and death.

*

"Must we go?" Even before the words are out, Will Draper knows he has no choice.

"Of course we must, Will," Miriam replies, as she examines yet another dress from her wardrobes. It is yellow silk, and adorned with pearls. "It will be like the old days, with Rafe and Mush trying to out jest one another, and Richard eating enough for an army. Master Tom will smile, and the world will be a happier place."

"He wants something," Will mutters. "The old devil always has some other motive. That last sojourn he took me on was supposed to be a restful break, yet I ended up investigating two murders."

"He did not know, when he asked you to go with him."

"He knew well enough." Will cannot explain everything to Miriam, but she suspects enough to know that Cromwell used her husband to remove an enemy. She does not know, and never will know, that Cromwell had murdered Sir Peregrine Martell, and let the blame pass onto another. "Who is paying for all the food?"

"Master Thomas has already sent that new fellow, Digby Waller around, with a purse of gold. More than enough."

"Digby Waller, you say?" Will's ears prick up. It is a name he has heard whispered, in connection with several unsavoury incidents, over the past months. "Then it is true. He works for Master Cromwell now?"

"I suppose he must." Miriam discards the yellow silk, and takes down a magnificent dark blue dress, that has a bodice encrusted with semi precious stones. "What of this one… a little too opulent, perhaps?"

"What does this fellow look like?"

"Who?"

"Digby Waller."

"Oh, Will, my darling man, you do not need to be so stuffy," Miriam replies, smiling at his pointed question. "The girls were present, and he behaved just like a gentleman should. Besides, he has a pox marked face, and is even younger than Mush."

"I am not jealous, my dear," Will reassures her. " You have my complete trust. I simply wish to know with whom Master Cromwell is associating, these days."

"Very well. He is as tall as you, though not as good looking. He has a flat nose, as if once broken in a fight, and long, mouse brown, hair. He dresses like a courtier, and tries to adopt the same sort of manners, but you can tell, easily, that he is of low birth."

"As once was I," Will reminds her.

"My grandmother's mother was a Babylonian princess," Miriam says, smiling cheekily. "Oh, how I have come down in this world, milord!"

"You mock me, madam?"

"I do, sir."

"It is not meet for a decent wife to treat her husband so," Will says.

"Then how shall I *decently* treat you … my dearest husband?" Miriam throws the dress aside, and gives him a pretty smile. "There is time enough, and little Gwyllam is asleep."

"Then let us make proper use of this bed, my girl," Will says.

"Take your muddy boots off first," Miriam tells him. "These sheets are Egyptian cotton, and cost us almost six pounds!"

"Six pounds?" Will pretends to be horrified. "How come you to have so much money to throw about on bed linen, madam?"

"I sold myself for a shilling a go," Miriam replies. "That is only one hundred and twenty times, sir."

"I have no shilling, girl."

"I shall give you a line on credit, sir,"

Miriam tells him. "Shall we start spending?"

"Then I shall be indebted to you for two shillings, forthwith, you wicked doxy!" Will pulls her into his arms, and feels the heat of her sudden passion. She pushes her tongue into his mouth, and clings, as if it was going to be the last time.

"It will give us an appetite for tonight," she says.

*

"Not that one, you idiot!" Ambassador Chapuys is almost at his wits end with his new servant. The man has come to him with good references, having worked for the royal household in Ghent, yet he seems incapable of even the simplest task. "The one with the pearl on the crown."

The young man, nods, and pads off to have another look for his master's best hat. He cannot understand all of the fuss, as the ambassador is only going next door for dinner. Since the invitation, the little Savoyard has been frantic about what to wear.

Eustace Chapuys is delighted with the invitation to dine with his old friend, Thomas Cromwell. It has been a while, and they have found themselves on different sides too often, but this is an opportunity to mend fences, and resume what was, for Chapuys, a close friendship.

"The purple cloak, I think," he mutters to himself. How much easier it would be, if only he had a wife to do such things for him. For a moment he allows himself to recall how Lady

Mary Boleyn had once offered herself to him, and how, like a fool, he had politely refused the offer.

Then there was Ilsa, whom had been his one true love, back in Savoy. Her early death, before they could marry had broken him for years, and made him wary of women for ever after. Still, there was the boy. His son would grow to maturity, and be cared for and provided with an income, despite never knowing his father.

"Here, master!" The servant appears, waving the correct hat, and Chapuys smiles at him. "Though the pearl seems to have fallen off!"

"God's teeth!" Eustace Chapuys curses. "Must I wear my second best hat?"

*

Digby Waller picks up the thick, silver chain, and fastens it about his wrist. It is more than a simple adornment, it is a way of concealing ready money about his person. Each link is worth a shilling, and there are twenty four links. Then he selects his smallest knife, and slips it up his left sleeve.

He has been taking lessons from Mush Draper, and has become quite good with a throwing knife. The young Jew is a patient teacher, and since joining the staff at Austin Friars, the two have taken to going about as a pair. They loiter about Cromwell's study, and are the first he calls on, these days.

Digby Waller can hardly believe his good fortune, having come from such a poor background. Orphaned at five, he has been raised by the servant of a well to do churchman, Friar Wilfred of Lambeth, who taught him to read and write well enough. It was only after being brought before Cromwell, for shouting abuse at Queen Anne, that his future has been assured.

The Privy Councillor had seemed to like him, and offered him a place at Austin Friars. Whilst still not one of the favoured inner circle, he hovers on the fringe, and is always ready to step up, when needed. It is this readiness, he thinks, that has earned him the honour of escorting Cromwell's gusts to Austin Friars. He, and Mush Draper are to go to the Elephant and Castle Inn, and bring Aldo Mercurius and his assistant safely to dinner.

"Ready, you coxcomb?" Mush says from the doorway.

"I am, Master Dandiprat," Digby Waller replies, and they both laugh. Such insults help them form a bond. He pushes a second knife into his belt, picks up his cudgel, and follows his friend out into the street.

"Dick will walk ahead, with a blazing torch," Mush says. "I fear we will make a pretty sight, and half the fools in London will follow."

"Let them," Waller replies, and swishes his club in an arc. "I am up to knocking a few heads, Mush."

"Then let us get on."

*

"Our escort awaits," Popo says. "Two young popinjays, with a torch bearer."

"Then let us be on our way," the alchemist replies. "Bring the cedar box along with you, Popo."

"Is that entirely wise?" the servant asks.

"Perhaps not, but I must have it." The alchemist has something in mind, but does not make his plans too obvious.

"And the powder?" Popo asks.

"Of course," the alchemist snaps at his assistant. "How else can I make gold?"

*

"You look very ... regal, father."

"Thank you George," Thomas Boleyn replies, as he straightens his cap on his head. "Scottish pearls, and gold thread on the collars. Even the king has not anything so fine."

"Then do not wear it in his presence," George tells his father.

"*Monsignour* is above such things," the father replies. "As the king's father-in-law, I am looked up to by all."

"Not by Cromwell," the son replies. "He is as like to poison your soup, father."

"He would not dare," the *Monsignour* says, haughtily. "To offer me personal violence is to offend the king."

"Perhaps, but I shall only eat from the common plates," George tells him. "I have no wish to turn blue, and choke my last at Austin Friars."

"Cromwell is not so crude." Monsignour fiddles with the ruff at his neck. "When he strikes, it will be subtle. He will try to show us up, as misusing the king's treasury, or some such thing."

"I don't know," says George Boleyn. "I still think it was he who put that damned rumour about, saying I was a … a sodomite. I have had to swive half the ladies in court to still that nonsense!"

"You are too suspicious," the father tells him. "Let us dine well, but use a long spoon … for we are supping with the devil!"

*

"I would rather serve the master's guests, than sit at table, my love," Rafe Sadler's lover, Ellen Barré, tells him. "Can I not be excused?"

"Master Cromwell invites you to dinner, my dear. It is a great honour," Rafe replies. "Miriam will be there, so that you might have someone to talk to. Then again, you like Will, and Richard, and neither Norfolk nor Suffolk will bite you."

"But the *other* lords…." Ellen Barré insists. "They are not to my taste, my dear."

"They are only Boleyns," Rafe says, soothingly. "They are not really noble. Why, *Monsignour's* own father was a low sort of a merchant, and his grandfather used to gather wood, and hawk kindling, for his living."

"And I am a servant." Ellen is adamant that she will be out of place.

"You are my betrothed," Rafe replies. "Master Cromwell shall have your husband declared legally dead, in a few more months. Soon you might find yourself to be a grand lady. The king takes note of me, and there might be a title coming my way. He knows that it was I who drafted the great Oath of Supremacy, and that it is I who will guide it through parliament, stage by stage."

"Then we will all have to swear?" The woman, who has known a poor husband once, distrusts vows, and oaths.

"Not women, of course. They have no legal say." Rafe Sadler tells his betrothed. "We are still working on other exceptions too, so that those who can be, are spared."

"Like Sir Thomas More?" Ellen Barré asks. She is fond of the old fellow, and dislikes the way he is being mistreated, for the sake of the new queen.

"Even Thomas Cromwell might not save that one." Rafe kisses her cheek. "Now, put on your best dress, my dearest one, and let us dine with these Boleyn rogues."

"Why does Master Cromwell invite them?"

"Politics, I suppose."

"They hate him." Ellen is worried for them all, and Rafe reassures her, with a smile.

"Master Tom says they hate *everyone*, so we are in good company, my love!"

4   The Alchemist

Miriam Draper, in her capacity as caterer, has excelled herself, Thomas Cromwell thinks. The great table is placed down the centre of the great hall, and has a linen runner going the full length, from end to end, and covering the centre of the oak top. Every couple of feet, there is a silver candlestick, of Flemish design, with real, wax candles, illuminating the room.

There is an engraved silver platter at each place, with a pewter goblet, and a fine glass, for wine. Set on either side of the silver platters, are a fairly new innovation to noble English diners: a sharp, bone handled knife, for cutting meat, and a triple tined silver fork, to help the food into the mouth, without resorting to ones fingers.

"Such splendour," Thomas Cromwell mutters. Then he claps his hands to attract one of the house servants. "James, you are to make a note of all the silverware, and make sure none of the guests take it away as a keepsake."

"As you say, Master Tom," the old man says. "Though Master Charles is back in funds, and will not pilfer."

"I think more of the Boleyn guests," Cromwell replies, with a smile. "It has cost me six hundred marks to set up this table, and that is without food on it. I want them dazzled by my wealth, not enriched by it. They must understand that I am worth as much as they. Have the servants dress in their very best Sunday clothes, and be at their most attentive."

"Of course, sir," James, who has been with

Cromwell for many years, has never known his master be so frivolous. In the past, he has always counselled caution where money is concerned. In the entrance hall Ellen Barré, and Rafe Sadler are waiting to greet the others. First to arrive, by palanquin, is Tom Howard, Duke of Norfolk.

"Damned womanly way to travel," he curses, as he steps through the door. "Only my bastard of a hunter threw me this morning, and I landed on my arse!"

"My Lord Norfolk, I am sorry to hear this. Are you discomfited?" Rafe asks, showing professional concern.

"Bruised arse. A cushion will do nicely, Sadler. I see the king has let you off for tonight. I say, who is this fine filly?"

"Mistress Ellen Barré, my betrothed, Your Lordship."

"Lucky beggar!" Norfolk leers, and stamps off into the main hall. "Am I early?" The servant, James, hurries forward, and pushes a goblet of red wine into his hand. "Ah, keep them coming, old fellow. Keep them coming!"

Richard hears the commotion, and descends the stairs. He espies Norfolk and goes over to him.

"My Lord Norfolk," he says. "Have you heard the one about the poxed whore and the bishop… no?" They sidle off, and Norfolk roars with laughter.

Will arrives a moment later, with Miriam on his arm. They throw off their cloaks, and join Richard and Norfolk. Charles Brandon is next, and comes galloping into the courtyard, as if the devil was on his tail. He jumps from the saddle, and almost runs into the house.

"God Bless all here," he says, and takes a glass of wine from one of the servants. "I thought I would not make it in time, Rafe. Is this the lady I hear so much of?"

"Mistress Ellen Barré, sir."

"Charmed." The Duke of Suffolk bows, and kisses Ellen's hand. "She matches Colonel Draper's wife in beauty, old fellow. I should keep her away from court. The king likes beautiful women, and thinks he can graze unfettered."

"He is married now," Ellen says.

"Of course," Suffolk says, and grins at Rafe's woman. "A man might have the rose, yet still wish to pick the odd wild flower.. eh?"

"If you would care to go through, Charles?" Thomas Cromwell appears, and ushers Suffolk into the great hall. "Are there more to come yet, Rafe?"

"We are waiting for… ah, here they come now."

"Cromwell!" George Boleyn nods his head, almost dismissively. "You know my father, do you not?"

"*Monsignour*," Cromwell bows as low as he dare, and still be able to straighten up. Yes, he thinks, that is the supercilious arse I once kicked out of Lambeth Palace. "My house is your house tonight. Pray, do go through, where your dear brother-in-law, Norfolk awaits."

"Oh, that old fool," George groans. "Is he as boorish as ever?" The Boleyns move inside, and almost at once, Eustace Chapuys is there in his best cap and gown. He holds out his hand to

Cromwell, and they embrace, warmly.

"Old friend, thank you for coming," Cromwell tells him.

"A pleasure, Thomas, though I see it is not to be an intimate dinner. Was that Boleyn I saw before me?"

"I regret so," Cromwell says, "but I will not sit you near them. The old fellow is so tedious these days. Ah, I see torches coming. I believe my guest of honour is here."

"Goodness, is it some Ottoman lord?" Chapuys catches sight of the extraordinarily begowned alchemist, and his fat little compatriot. They are decked out in silks, and on his head, Mercurius has a conical hat, trimmed with huge feathers. "Such a magnificent hat!"

"Ostrich feathers," Popo explains, as he bows to Chapuys, in mistake for Cromwell.

"Have I the honour of addressing Lord Cromwell?"

"This is he," Chapuys says, stepping to one side.

"Then, on my honour, good lord, I am presenting to you, Aldo Mercurius, Alchemist Royal to Prince Ygor of Lithuania!"

"I am pleased to meet you," Cromwell says. "And you are Master Popo, his assistant?"

"Secretary, assistant, and principal disciple," Popo replies, bowing again. "We eat, yes?"

"We do, please come inside." The room falls into silence as the alchemist makes his appearance. It is Norfolk who first finds words to utter.

"What is this, Cromwell, are we dining with Turcomen now?" He laughs, but none join in.

"May I name, Grand Master Aldo Mercurius, Alchemist Royal to the Prince of Lithuania." Thomas Cromwell gestures to the table. "Let us be seated, my friends, for there is a magnificent feast to get through!"

Rafe Sadler knows whom dislikes whom, and nudges them all into reasonably acceptable places. Only the alchemist seems unwilling to take his place of honour, beside Thomas Cromwell.

"Do sit, Grand Master Aldo," Cromwell urges, but the alchemist makes a criss-cross gesture with his hands, and mutters in a mixture of Latin, and an unknown language.

"I dare not," he says, in a thick, north European accent. "Can you not see how many we are?"

Thomas Cromwell takes a quick head count, and groans at the appalling oversight.

"Thirteen," the alchemist says, with dread in his voice. "We are thirteen, and that will not do. Bring me salt, at once!" James hurries forward with a silver bowl, and the alchemist takes it from him. He chants, in the same, strange, unknown language, and sprinkles the salt across the table.

"That is not Latin, sir?" Chapuys asks.

"Chaldean," the alchemist replies. "It is most beneficial in these cases. There will be no ill luck around this table now."

Almost at once, there is a loud knocking at the door. James scurries to answer the knock, and returns, in quick time, with a tall, good looking man at his shoulder.

"My pardon, dear Master Thomas," Tom Wyatt says, bowing to Cromwell, "but I thought to beg a bite of convivial supper. I see that I intrude, and I shall withdraw at once, dear sir."

"No, you will not, Master Wyatt," Thomas Cromwell says, happily. The dissolute court poet, and diplomat, is there, as if by magic, and saves the evening. "Draw up a chair, and you shall make us up to fourteen, my friend. Later, you shall sing for your supper, no doubt."

"The trick is trying to stop me, Master Cromwell," Tom Wyatt says. "I say, is that you George, you old roisterer? Still giving it to poor old Suffolk's mistress, whenever his back is ... Oh, hello there, Charles... I did not see you behind Norfolk. Do forgive my jest... I spoke out of turn."

"As always," Suffolk replies, with a charming smile. "I fear you bell poor Boleyn with your own crime. Is there a lady safe from your attentions in London?"

"Not in the world, Charles," Wyatt says. He affects to be a little drunker than he is, as it acts as a useful cover for the times his tongue works before he has thought. "Why, Colonel Draper will regale you with tales of our adventures in Venice, and Rome. Whilst he stabbed the men, I afforded a similar service to their women."

"I am pleased it was not the other way around, Tom," Miriam says. "For he was away a long time."

"Ah, Miriam... I did not ... Perhaps I should look about the table, and see who else is here that I must avoid offending. Good God, sir, I did not know it was fancy dress!"

"Aldo Mercurius, sir," the alchemist says,

softly. "I wear the dress of my profession."

"Juggler?"

"Alchemist."

"Ah, you are the entertainment," Wyatt says, and giggles foolishly. "Will the rabbit come on a dish tonight, or from up your sleeve, Master Mercurius?"

"Manners, Wyatt," Cromwell mutters.

"Do not worry on my account, Master Cromwell," Mercurius tells his host. "I am armed with the power of alchemy, and can perform feats beyond the normal knowledge of mere mortals."

"Excellent," Wyatt says, with a supercilious grin plastered to his face. "I divine that the first course is here. Is that Miriam's famous peppered hare stew I smell?"

"Talented, as well as beautiful," George Boleyn mutters to his father. "I wonder which is more tasty… she, or the soup?"

"That is a matter of taste," Aldo Mercurius says, from the further end of the table. George, who has scarcely whispered, is shocked, and stares at the stranger in their midst. The alchemist smiles, and taps a finger to his forehead. "The power of thought, George Boleyn. From your mind, to mine. It is a curse."

"It is horse shit," Tom Wyatt whispers to Richard Cromwell, who cannot help but laugh.

"Ah you doubt my powers, little poet?" Aldo Mercurius leans over and says something into Cromwell's ear. The Privy Councillor nods, and claps for his servant.

"James, bring ink, quill and paper for the Grand Master," he says. "For he wishes to make a small demonstration of his power. With My Lords' permissions?"

"Ah, magic!" Norfolk says, through a mouthful of peppered hare stew. "Good show, Cromwell. You know how to entertain a fellow, and no mistake." Despite everything, Norfolk likes his host, and does not look forward to the day when they must clash. He will take no pleasure in sending the man to his death, but politics can be a hard world to inhabit.

The assistant, Popo, takes three sheets of paper, and tears each of them carefully into four pieces. He lays a piece out before each guest, and takes up the ink and quill. His master closes his eyes, and appears to slip into a trance like state.

"I will pass amongst you," Popo says. "Let each one here write their name, and a question they wish answered. Then fold your papers, and place them on this dish. The Grand Master will divine, by touch, and answer where he can."

"Me first," Tom Wyatt says, and snatches the quill. A few minutes later, and all have done as they have been told. Popo takes the platter of folded papers, and stands by the roaring fire. The alchemist stands, and with eyes still closed, crosses to his servant. The table falls silent as he hovers his hand over the plate.

"No touching, Master Magician," George Boleyn calls, and they all laugh. The alchemist does as he is bidden, and keeps his eyes closed.

"Ah, a sensible question, sir!" Aldo Mercurius opens his eyes, and turns his gaze onto Thomas Cromwell, who stares back, stone faced.

"You look at me, sir, but you do not…"

"The price will hold," Mercurius says. "Seventeen shillings a bushel. Is that what you wish to know?" He picks up the top paper, opens it, and nods. "Cromwell ... what price will ..."

"A bushel of corn be, this summer," Cromwell finishes. He stares, open mouthed at his guests, and a murmur runs about the room. The alchemist tosses the opened note into the fire, and touches the second in the pile.

"Really, Master Wyatt!" the alchemist says. "Is the word 'arse' a question, or a description of your oafish manner?"

"Jesus!" Tom Wyatt blushes, for it is what he has written beneath his name. The second question goes into the flames, and the third is touched.

"Ah, a lady." Mercurius smiles. "Good manners forbids me to reveal your question ... but the answer is ... yes, soon." Miriam claps her hands in delight.

"That is my question," she says. "Thank you, Grand Master."

"Now, here is a man who likes to play with fire." Aldo Mercurius picks up the next question. "I fear that this is bordering on treason, sir. Shall I name you, and answer?"

"Burn it!" Thomas Boleyn almost leaps from his seat. He has been foolish, and the paper can cost him his head.

"As you wish." The paper goes onto the fire. "Next, we have another lady. Fear not, Mistress Barré, it will come to pass, perhaps even more often than you wish." Ellen Barré blushes, and nods her thanks. "The next question is ... ah, one for me, Ambassador Chapuys. As you use your official title, and write in Latin, I will answer in the same way, shall I?"

Eustace Chapuys claps his hands in delight, and shakes his head. His question is flippant, and not one that could be guessed at.

"English will do, sir," he says, bowing in respect.

"Which ever language I choose, I fear I must disappoint you, lest you have a fast galley at your disposal. The feathers you admire are ostrich, and cannot be found in England. Popo discovered mine in far off Barbary."

"No matter," Chapuys, whose sartorial taste is questionable, replies. "Though they are such *magnificent* adornments."

"Then you shall have my spares," Aldo Mercurius says, and the little Savoyard almost feints with joy. The demonstration continues in a similar vein, until the last of the dozen questions is burnt to ashes. The room is stunned by such an amazing display of magic, and they look from one to another to see if any has an explanation.

"Can you see through paper?" Rafe asks. He is sure it is a trick, but cannot discern how it was done.

"Still you do not believe?" Mercurius shakes his head. "It is important that each person touches the paper. Their life force impregnates the sheet, and the image of that person comes into my mind. Once I know who has written the question, I cast out my thoughts, to mingle with theirs. Usually, the question is still in their mind, and I '*see*' it, as clear as day."

"And this always works?" Thomas

Cromwell asks.

"I must be in a safe environment." The alchemist returns to his meal. "Once, a lord in Hungary set me by an Infidel ambassador, so that I might perceive his secrets, but I failed. If I am hungry, frightened, or tired, it does not work. The same applies to personal readings. If the stars are not right, my powers are lessened."

"Then you swear it is a real power?" Richard Cromwell demands.

"Think of a number between one and twelve, Master Ogre," the alchemist says. "Do you have one?"

"Yes."

"Say it out loud."

"Seven." The alchemist holds up his right palm, to show that it is empty. Then he clenches it into a fist, and makes several rapid passes through the air. He opens the hand, to show a crumpled piece of parchment, no bigger than a couple of inches square.

"For you, Master Richard." The big bear of a man grunts, and snatches at the paper. He opens it, and gasps. The number seven is scrawled on it. "Whenever you stop believing, look upon this!"

"More!" Norfolk shouts, and slaps the table. "By God, Cromwell, but this fellow is a treat!"

"I came as Master Cromwell's guest," Mercurius snaps. "Not as some faker of magic tricks. I am a true alchemist, born under the most auspicious signs, my Lord Norfolk. I have spent twenty years learning the greatest secret of the age, and am almost there. I do not do after dinner 'tricks', sir!"

"Then tell my fortune, you knave!"

"That is a small thing," Mercurius says, stiffly. "For a block head, shall finish on a block."

"Eh, what is that supposed to mean?" Norfolk sinks down into his seat, and frowns at the riddle.

"What secret do you speak of, sir?" Cromwell asks.

"What else?" Aldo Mercurius straightens himself to his full height, and makes a sign in the air. "Transmutation."

"You have the stone?" Thomas Cromwell almost bites the words back. "We *must* talk, later."

"Not so fast, Master Cromwell," *Monsignour* says. "What stone is this you speak of, good sir?"

"It is nothing, My Lord." Cromwell waves for the servants to recharge their glasses.

"You speak of the philosopher's stone, do you not?" the older Boleyn says. "Am I right?"

"It is just a dream," Cromwell says.

"A dream?" Aldo Mercurius sneers. "I am the greatest alchemist of the age, Master Cromwell, and I assure you, it is no dream. I can turn base metal into gold!"

"Gold?" Suffolk and Norfolk say together.

"Then prove it," *Monsignour* Boleyn demands.

"One moment, sir," Miriam says. "There are another eight courses to come. I will not have such fine food wasted. If Grand Master Mercurius can make gold, then let him do it after we have eaten."

"Well said," Will Draper says, supportively. "The fellow works best on a full stomach, did he not just say?"

"I have never heard such…"

"Horse shit, Master Wyatt?" Popo says, sniggering at the poet's discomfort. "Scoff all you wish, but I am here to tell you all, as God is my witness… I have seen it."

"Then we shall eat," George says, "and discover the truth of this matter later. The stew was wonderful, Lady Miriam, and I look forward to the remainder of the feast."

"I am no Lady, sir," Miriam says.

"Then you are a mistress," George says, and casts a sidelong look at Will Draper. His intention is to put a doubt in the fellow's mind, and make him wonder if it is more than just Suffolk's mistress he is swiving. He hopes to prick his foe into doubting his own wife.

Will understands, and silently reserves the right to give the younger Boleyn a good thrashing, at the first opportunity. He is aware of his loutish behaviour at court, and still has his doubts over George's sexuality. The man protests his innocence by sleeping with any woman who will have him, except his wife.

"She is my mistress, Boleyn," he retorts. "As Suffolk has his mistress … and your own good wife."

"What's that?" George's face glows red. He has been suspicious for a while, and finds his wife's interest in Charles Brandon personally insulting.

"Why, I say sir, that we all have our ladies," Will says with a frown. "How is the health of your good lady?"

"Do you bait me, Draper?" Boleyn leans forward, and touches a finger to his belt, where an ornate dagger hangs.

"Do you call me out, sir?" Will Draper senses the table go quiet. Then the alchemist raises his hands, and speaks.

"Have a care, my dear Lord Rochford," he intones at George Boleyn, "for I foresee an empty place at table, and a beautiful widow who will not grieve."

The prediction makes George hold his tongue. He is a competent swordsman, but he knows that to call out Will Draper is to court certain death. He will keep silent, and deal with his enemy in a safer way. London is a dangerous city, and even the best of men have been struck down from some dark shadow.

"Come, eat up," Tom Howard, Duke of Norfolk bellows. "I will see this man do miracles this night. Gold, by God … Gold!"

5   The Transmutation

The final course, custard tarts, scented with rose petals, remains only half eaten. The consecutive platters of hare, broiled chicken in cream, roasted cuts of Spring lamb, beef, and pork, chestnut stuffed quails, turbot, roast swan, and eels, poached in milk, have taken their toll, and the company concludes the feast with goblets of the best Italian wine.

"I am fit to burst my breeches," Norfolk says, and belches loudly. "Your pardon, Miriam."

"A rare compliment to the food, my dearest Lord Norfolk," Miriam says.

"Come now, call me Tom, or Uncle Norfolk if you will, my sweet girl," Norfolk replies. "If you ever leave that rascal Draper, come to me, and I will treat you like a real lady."

"My Lord, can even you manage three mistresses … and a wife too?"

"Bugger my wife," Norfolk curses. "I wish *someone* would, for the old mare makes my life an utter misery."

"What, even from her separate castle, sir?" Will Draper says. He knows the Lady Norfolk, and finds her to be a most attractive, though dangerous woman.

"Ah, Colonel Draper, I was just trying to seduce your lovely wife away from you. You are a lucky man, old fellow."

"As are you, sir," Will replies. "Miriam carries a castrating knife concealed in her dress, and has unmanned other men before you."

"Dear Christ!" Norfolk winces, and moves a

hand to cover his codpiece. "You mean ...?"

"What do you think I put in the stew, sir?" Miriam says, and the duke bursts into laughter.

"Let us be down to it," *Monsignour* demands. "I will see gold tonight, or have this fellow's back flayed!"

"The Grand Master is my guest, Boleyn," says Cromwell. "It is for me to say who shall go punished, or unpunished, under my roof. Just as it is for the master to kick the dog's arse!"

"You dare insult me?" the older Boleyn says. Since his elevation to becoming father-in-law of the king, he finds any kind of opposition to his will to be infuriating.

"Insult you, *Monsignour*?" Cromwell spreads his hands, as if to indicate his complete surprise. "What have you to do with the kicking of dog's ... ah, I see. You hold an old grudge against me, for doing my sworn duty, sir?"

"You enjoyed it!" *Monsignour* hisses.

"I was Cardinal Wolsey's man, sir," Cromwell says, "and you offered him an insult. He had to serve you back in the same way. I was his instrument."

"But you *enjoyed* it!"

"Of course. I *always* enjoyed serving the great Cardinal Wolsey, sir," Thomas Cromwell replies, lightly. "Now, shall we get on?"

"Yes, damn it," George Boleyn says. "If this fellow speaks the truth, we are all made men. Imagine knowing how to work such magic!"

"To what end, George?" Thomas Cromwell sneers. "Would you make enough gold to make you the richest man in the world?"

"Why not?" George cannot see why he could not have rooms filled with gold. The idea makes him heady with power.

"Because it would be worthless," Rafe Sadler puts in.

"There speaks a wise man," Tom Wyatt says. "Imagine if each man in this room could make all the gold he could? Why it would be like a half penny loaf for a farthing."

"You are talking in riddles," George Boleyn snaps.

"Only to you, George … only to you." Cromwell sighs, and explains, as a tutor to a child. "Imagine that there is a million pounds of gold in the world, and someone finds a million more, overnight. Then the first million is worth only half as much. Therefore, if there is one million, and we make another ten… our gold is worth that much less."

"Exactly," Chapuys mutters, listening to the lively exchanges. He will have much to write to the emperor about, in his next official letter.

"Then what do you propose?" *Monsignour* demands.

"Propose?" Thomas Cromwell smiles. "Why, nothing sir, for there is no magic in the world that can turn turnips into carrots… as there is nothing that can turn base metal into gold!"

"The Grand Master knows how," Popo says, quietly from a corner of the room. George Boleyn is the only one to hear this, and sidle over to the magician's assistant.

"Tell me true," he asks. "Can it be done?"

"In a small way," Popo replies, softly. "I

think there are too many here for so fine a secret. Methinks Grand Master Mercurius will find it all too much for him."

"If not, I will have his secret." George taps the heavy purse at his belt. "Perhaps we can come to an understanding?"

"I would dearly love to accept your bribe, sir," Popo says, but the secret is in my master's head. It is he you must bring over to your way of thinking."

"Would he take a bribe?"

"Of gold?" Popo smiles. "Why, when he can make his own gold. The machine is small, and makes only enough for our daily needs, but if there were a grander…"

"Behold!" George spins around, to see that Aldo Mercurius has cleared one end of the table. He takes a green cloth from inside his gown, and spreads it across the oak surface. Next, he takes from his loose sleeve, a cedar wood box, and places it on the cloth. "Popo, bring the powder. Hurry man, the moon will not stay this bright all night!"

Popo sighs, and produces a small velvet bag. He holds it up for all to see, before depositing it next to the box. Mercurius beckons for all those interested to draw nearer, and most of the men crowd in to watch.

"My *aparatus diaboli* awaits." He smiles at them, noting the greed stamped on several faces. "Yes, my devil's machine, gentlemen. It holds the power of the cosmos within its workings, and can turn powdered lead into gold."

"Must it be lead?" George asks.

"Lead is the only element heavy enough," Mercurius explains. "One can hardly make golden feathers. You see, that was where all the others went wrong. Each element has its place, and lead is next to gold in the cosmic list."

"How does it change into gold?" Cromwell asks. "I confess I am dubious, Grand Master."

"That is perfectly understandable," Mercurius replies. "How many charlatans have pretended to knowledge they do not possess?"

"Enough," Rafe Sadler says. "The last one was hanged, I believe."

"Do you understand that everything is made of the same thing?" Mercurius asks his audience. There are several blank looks, so he explains. "When the Creator made the world in seven days, he used Himself, for there was nothing else. He took of Himself, and made the earth and the sky, and all the things upon the face of the waters."

"Then God is in everything?" Miriam asks.

"Of course. Therefore, it follows that we are all made of the same matter. This matter, I call 'flux'." Mercurius intertwines his fingers. "Put the flux together so … and we have wood, so … and it is soil, manure, or water. One has only to know how to break down the flux, and put it back together in another way, and you can make anything."

"And the box?" Thomas Cromwell is becoming interested.

"An intricate little device, containing a precise clockwork movement," the alchemist tells the audience. "Small cogs fit within frames, and twist apart the lead, until it is primeval flux. This then passes through an internal compartment, that holds certain fluids, where the flux is purified, and allowed to settle back into another form."

"It turns into gold?" *Monsignour* asks.

"Eventually," Popo puts in, "but it is a damnably intricate process, and the Grand Master's box can make but a few grains in a night. It has to be night, else the formulae do not work."

"A minor matter," Mercurius says, casting a doleful look at his assistant. "My *transmutator* works, but on a small scale. If I could make the *aparatus* on a much larger scale, it would alter flux on a better ratio. This small engine cost me my fortune to build."

"But it works?" Thomas Cromwell looks around the table. He sees that Norfolk, Suffolk, and both Boleyns are calculating how they might benefit.

"Of course it does." The alchemist slides open a slot in the box, and tips in a thimble full of powdered lead. He closes the aperture, and produces a small key, which he inserts into a hole on the side of the box. He turns it, several times, and there is an audible clicking noise from within. "There, it is set. Now, we must wait for an hour or two. Might I trouble you for more wine, Master Cromwell, whilst we all wait?"

The two women become bored quickly, and retire for the night. Norfolk tries to match Tom Wyatt drink for drink, and soon passes out in his chair. Suffolk stays awake, and keeps a wary eye on the magical box. The alchemist spends the time entertaining Thomas Cromwell, and the Boleyns, with vanishing coins, and clever card tricks. Rafe stokes the fire, and ponders all he has witnessed that evening.

Will Draper escorts Miriam to a borrowed bedroom, and excuses himself for a while. She tries to entice him into the bed, but he insists on returning to the great hall.

"I must see this out, my love," he says. "There is something afoot, and I cannot rest, until I am at the root of it."

"We Jews are a race of mystics," Miriam says. "It does not interest me. Grandfather used to read about such things, and always maintained that it was for God alone to know about these matters."

"Then you do not believe this alchemist?"

"It matters not to me, husband," she explains. "Our business has made us rich beyond measure. I have no need of gold made from turnips."

"Lead," Will says, correcting her. "He uses lead. It all seems so … plausible. I watched his every move with the questions, and could see no hint of trickery."

"That is when you must be most wary," Miriam says. "For a clever rogue knows that some truth is a powerful tool. Now go, and see lead turn into gold. Promise me but one single thing, my dearest husband."

"Yes?"

"Do not buy this fabulous *apparatus*, without speaking to me first." Miriam kisses him then, and he is tempted to stay. Her body comes to him, as if drawn, and he touches her skin in awe.

"What question did you ask of him?" Will asks.

"Hurry back, and I will whisper it in your ear."

*

"It is time." Grand Master Aldo Mercurius, Alchemist Royal to Prince Ygor of Lithuania, crosses to the table, and taps the cedar wood box with his knuckles. It whirs once, then remains silent. "A sheet of paper please, Master Cromwell."

The paper is laid beside the box. Mercurius picks the box up, and moves his fingers over one edge. There is a click, and a small panel slides open. The alchemist tips the box on its edge, and shakes. To the gasps of all, a trickle of golden dust cascades out onto the paper.

"It is scarcely enough to make a lady's ring," George Boleyn moans.

"True enough," Tom Wyatt says, "but what if this wondrous box were a hundred times larger?"

The Boleyns exchange a glance. Thomas Cromwell examines the gold powder, and nods his head. He confirms that it is real, and assesses its value.

"With these amounts, the box might produce enough to keep a gentleman in small comfort." He turns to Mercurius. "You have spent your fortune making a clever toy, Grand Master."

"Alas, yes," the alchemist confesses. "I have spent over ten thousand Ducats on my transmutator, and had but a thousand back. It will take me twenty years to get back to where I started. Even Prince Ygor would not fund me any longer. That is why I now travel the known, and the unknown, world."

"How much would it take to build a box big enough to change sheets of lead at a time?" George Boleyn asks.

"Oh that it were so easy," Popo says. "It is a dream, gentlemen. Fifty thousand pounds would build the box, but before that, there would be other things."

"Enough, Popo," the alchemist warns.

"There are the special fluids, which must be brought from the far off Spice Islands, and then we would need a huge grinder, for the lead powder. It must be milled by moonlight … or did I not mention that earlier?"

"Why?" Cromwell asks.

"God knows," Popo replies. The Grand Master will not tell me that part of the ritual."

"Then it is magical?" *Monsignour* asks.

"Everything is magical, until you understand the science of it, sir," Mercurius says. "The moon affects our moods, and makes the tides of the great ocean rise, and fall. It seems that this same moonlight helps the process. I know not how."

"Then it can be done?" Old Boleyn is fascinated. Like Cromwell, he knows that too much gold will ruin a country, but regular extra amounts will not be noticed, and can make a man richer than the Roman emperors of ancient times.

"For about seventy, or seventy five thousand pounds," Aldo Mercurius, the alchemist admits. "But who, in all the world can find so much money? It would take the ten wealthiest men in England to gather such wealth at short notice."

"Perhaps we could discuss this further," Cromwell replies. "I can raise a portion, and these gentlemen, together, might contribute. What say you, Boleyn, shall we form a company, and each take a part of the wealth?"

"I think not, Master Cromwell," Thomas Boleyn says.

"But father…"

"Enough, George, I say. It is an idle dream. Seventy five thousand pounds is a ridiculous sum of money, far beyond anything one man … even a rich one… could raise."

"I suppose you are right, *Monsignour*," Thomas Cromwell admits. "Though, imagine the power. We could control the world's economy with such an *apparatus*. Nations would bow down to us, and we would be richer than …"

"The king?" Rafe Sadler says. There is an uncomfortable silence, as each man ponders the traitorous thought. "We will do well to forget this demonstration, Master Cromwell. It will come to no good."

"Henry would ruin us." Suffolk shifts uneasily in his chair, and looks to Thomas Cromwell for guidance.

"A fool's dream," Cromwell confirms. "Let us resolve never to speak of this again. Master Mercurius, we thank you for your remarkably entertaining demonstration, and wish you well with your … toy."

"*Let lips be closed,
our words to hold,
lest we lose our heads,
o'er devil's gold.*"

Tom Wyatt's couplet seems to have a sobering effect, and the party begins to break up. Cromwell calls for Norfolk's palanquin to be brought into the courtyard, and asks Rafe Sadler to see Eustace Chapuys safely back to his house, next door.

"Do you need men to see you home, Lord Suffolk?"

"I have a mind to visit some lower house, sir," Charles Brandon replies, patting his full purse. "For I find I am in funds again."

"May you never lack for silver, sir," Thomas Cromwell says. "As long as you have friends, you will prosper. Good night to you, My Lord." He glances about, and sees that the Boleyns' toughs have arrived, and will see their masters safely away. "Master Waller!"

"At your service, sir," Digby Waller says, stepping from the shadows. "Pray, escort the Grand Master back to his lodgings. Take Mush with you."

"The rogue is asleep under the kitchen table," Waller says, with an affectionate smile. "Let him rest, and I will take these gentlemen off. They will be safe enough with me."

"Then God's speed to you." Cromwell pats the young man on his shoulder, and turns to retreat within. Those who are staying overnight are all abed, save Will Draper, who watches from a quiet corner of the hall. He recalls a time, not too distant, when Thomas Cromwell treated him with such open friendship, and it saddens him that they are no longer so close.

He wonders when they shall ever be friends

again, and wanders off to find his wife. Miriam is asleep, but awakens the moment he slips into bed.

"Did it work?" she mumbles.

"It did," Will replies, cuddling into her. "Though God alone knows why!"

*

The streets are quiet, save for the occasional night watchman about his duties, and Digby Waller has no trouble in getting the alchemist and his assistant safely back to the Elephant and Castle Inn. The inn keeper is still up, and ready to serve them a nightcap.

"Will you stay a while, and have a hot, mulled wine, Master Waller?" Mercurius asks.

"Why not?"

"Excellent. Then you can discharge your duty, as instructed, and we can all go to our beds happy."

"My duty, sir?"

"Come now," the alchemist says, giving a knowing smile to Popo. "Must I touch your palm, and divine what is in your mind, young man?"

Digby Waller pulls his hands away, and places them behind his back, away from any magical touch. He tries to close his thoughts to the man, but decides it is futile. For how can you ever know what the man can truly divine?

"Then you know what is in my mind?"

"That which is put there by your master."

"Then I do not need to speak."

"No, you do not... save for the details," Mercurius replies. "I do not '*see*' the where, or the when. Your mind is chaotic, my boy."

"I will bring you to my master, tomorrow."

"When he will make me such an offer, as cannot be refused?"

"That is not my business, sir," Waller says. "I am instructed to tell you only this. The money can be found. How long will it take, and can it be done in secret?"

"Three months," Mercurius tells him. "Though it cannot be done in secret in London. Every great lord has his spies, and the king has men to seek out such things."

"Colonel Draper, you mean?"

"I do. There is a man who must be kept busy, else he will sniff us out, Master Waller."

"He shall be taken care of."

"I will have nothing to do with murder!" The alchemist is aghast at the thought of it.

"God, no!" Digby Waller throws his hands up in horror. "The king shall discover some task which the man must attend to. It might be in Ireland, or Scotland, but he will be kept away from court, until it is too late."

"Then we must find a secret place, away from here." Mercurius turns to Popo, who nods.

"Somewhere on the coast," the assistant replies. "A quiet port, where the shipments of special oils, and spices can be brought in, without notice."

"Secrecy is of the uttermost importance," Digby says. His instructions are clear, and his master will brook no errors. "Put it about that you will tour the northern towns, and slip away. I will keep in touch with you, and I alone. If any other comes to you, they mean to play you false. Trust no-one, save me, and my master."

"Very well. Now, my price."

"Seventy five thousand pounds."

"That is to make my *apparatus* work, sir." Mercurius steeples his fingers, and smiles benignly. "I will have one fifth of all we produce."

"The master said you would speak thus," Digby Waller replies, "and he charges me to offer you a tenth part. If you wish to refuse this offer, then I must suggest that you read my mind."

Aldo Mercurius nods his acceptance. There is no point in demanding that which will turn these people against him. For a tenth, they will settle, but for a fifth, they might consider cutting his throat instead, once the machine is built.

"Let us shake hands on it," he says, and they clasp hands. The alchemist groans then, and shakes his head, as if groggy from too much good wine. "Take care, Master Waller, for I see a terrible end awaiting you!"

"What?" Digby Waller snatches his hand away, as if it were on fire. "Are you mad?"

"Forgive me, my dear young fellow," Aldo Mercurius says, as he wipes at his eyes with one, voluminous sleeve. "It is the overuse of sulphur, and other such chemicals. It sometimes makes me utter the most ridiculous nonsense."

6 Plots

The moors to the south of York are dotted with flocks of sheep, and tiny hamlets, where Catholicism still rules, and stubborn men refuse to forsake what is, to them, the true faith. They band together, in secret cabals, and attend a Mass, whenever it can be arranged.

Finding a priest to uphold the old ways is becoming increasingly harder, and those recalcitrants who still follow Rome lead a vagabond existence, wandering from village to village, where the misguided few hide them in secret places. It is to this bleak landscape that Will Draper is despatched, with orders to track down those miscreants, who will not swear loyalty to King Henry, and his new way of worship.

The commission has come directly from the king, and Will is mystified by it. Usually, his tasks are suggested by either Cromwell, or one of the others who are close to the king, but Henry has written his orders out with his own hand, and appended the royal seal.

So, Will has packed his belongings, saddled Moll, and set off north. He is to be away from the beginning of May, until the end of August, and does not look forward to life without his wife.

"Your business will take you far and wide," Miriam says. "As will mine. I have a mind to visit the northern ports, where my cogs, and ships, often put in. Might we not agree to meet up on our various travels?"

"A good idea, my love," Will replies. "I have business in York, Ripon, Whitby, and all down the east coast. Let us arrange matters, so that we see one another, every week or two."

Looking back, Will sees that it was a fine idea, and the visits with Miriam has kept his spirits up these last months. With only visits to Skipton and Helmsley left, he has little to show for all his efforts. In three and a half months, he has found a handful of women and a couple of men, still following Rome.

Will is not an inquisitor, and his orders are to bring these people into line, not persecute them. It is an easy matter for him to meet with the poor misguided folk, and give them a lurid description of the fate that awaits transgressors. By the time he has explained the workings of the torturer in the Tower of London, and the agonies of the stake, or being hanged, drawn and quartered, they are only too willing to convert to the new church.

"Return to your old ways, and there will be no second chance," Will tells them. "If the king comes, it will be with a sword in one hand, and a flaming torch in the other!"

Two more calls, to display Henry's new Royal Examiner, and his power, and he can ride home, happy that his task is complete. It is after Helmsley, and on the road to Skipton, that things start to go awry.

He is a mile short of the town, and its huge, fortified castle, when two riders come galloping towards him. Will slows Moll to a gentle amble, and loosens the pistol hanging from his pommel in its holster. The two riders also slow, and the older man waves, to show he is unarmed. Will canters forward.

"Good day, good sirs," he says, warily. The men look like father and son, and they are of the merchant class, from the cut of their clothes. "Might I name myself? I am Colonel Will Draper, the King's Examiner, and I am on a tour for His Majesty."

"God save the king," the younger fellow replies. "I am John Beckshaw, and this is my father, Joshua. He is a leading member of the town council, and acts as a magistrate for the county."

"Then we are well met, sir," Will says, bowing in the saddle. "I require a bed for a few nights, and your assurances that Skipton is for the new English church."

"That I cannot give, Colonel Draper," Joshua Beckshaw replies, with tears in his eyes. "I have known of your coming this se'night, and have been living in fear. There are those on the council who mutter about allegiance to Rome. They speak of Pope Clement being God's kinsman, and turn the common folk to the old religion at every opportunity."

"This is shocking news, sir," Will says. Indeed, it is, he thinks, for he is but one man, and town councillors often have men at arms to support them. It would be an easy matter to hang the King's Examiner, and raise a rebellion. "How many are they?"

"Three, but they command the Town Watchmen, and employ a dozen or more roughs, ready to crack heads." John Beckshaw explains. "We are merchants, sir, and know nothing of fighting."

"Who holds the castle?"

"Henry, First Earl of Cumberland, sir," Joshua explains. "He is the king's man, to his very marrow, but is raiding along the Scottish borderlands this season. He and My Lord Percy, the Duke of Northumberland, are intent on knocking a few Scots heads together. The castle is garrisoned by a few very old soldiers, and some servants."

"Will they fight?"

"Bless me, sir," Joshua exclaims. "I doubt they will even open the gate to us!"

"Then I must meet these fellows, and frighten them into submission," Will says with more courage than he feels.

"There is worse," John Beckshaw adds. "Things were quiet until ten days ago. We were all for Henry, and ready to worship as the king demands of us, when the priest came."

"What priest?" Will is suddenly alert. There have been rumours on his travels. "A tall man, built like a blacksmith, and breathing fire?"

"Yes, that is he. He claims to be a priest, but he carries a great axe in his belt, and curses us all with damnation, if we do not bow to Rome." the younger man says. "I do not want to go back to those days, sir, and will ride with you."

"Can you handle a pistol, or a sword, lad?"

"I can try."

"Good fellow. Where are these scoundrels now, Master Joshua?"

"Marching up and down, outside the castle's gate," the merchant replies. "The priest is demanding entrance. Once inside, he will be able to dominate the whole of North Yorkshire, and every fool in Christendom who still loves Rome, will flock to him."

"Will the garrison hold out?"

"There is a good well inside, and plenty of food," John tells Will, "but if some are still Roman Catholic, they might betray their lord."

"Then we must act, now." Will passes one of his pistols to the son, and explains its use. "Draw this back, point, and pull this trigger. If you must fire, get as close as you can, and do not close your eyes!"

"Sir, do not get my son killed," Joshua Beckshaw begs. "He is all I have in the world."

"Fear not, Master Beckshaw," Will replies, checking his second pistol. "I am the King's Examiner, and no man will withstand me."

"The priest is a giant," John mutters. "He speaks in a strange tongue, which I believe is Irish."

"Perhaps," Will says. Ireland is slow to bow to the new church, and the country is overflowing with hellfire priests, ready to swarm across England, for their cause. "I have a way with Irish rebels, and that is all this fellow is. He preaches against the king, that is treason. Come, let us ride. Master Joshua, pray slip into the town by another road, and raise all you can against this Catholic devil. Have them take up any weapon they can, and come to the castle."

"They are not fighters, sir!"

"They need do nothing, until the moment is right," Will explains. "I shall order this priest's followers to surrender. Have your friends shout for the king, and wave their scythes, and their axes in the air. Seeing that they are not for the pope, but against the king will unnerve the priest's followers. For none will wish to be called a traitor."

*

"Open the gate, or I will call down the damnation of Christ on all within!" The priest, a huge Irishman from the bleak Cork countryside, is full of self righteous anger, and he is quite prepared to conjure up a host of demons if need be, to terrorise the castle's sadly depleted garrison.

"Bugger off!" The retort comes from the battlements, and it is followed, closely, by a bucket full of stale urine, which splashes just short of the priest's feet. "This is the Earl of Cumberland's domain, not the bastard pope's!"

"Then we will tear down your gates, and destroy you all," the priest shouts back. He has a crowd of about fifty men with him, and less than half are armed with spears and axes. If he is to get into the fortress, he must rely on the power of God's Will. He starts to curse in Latin, and urges his followers to storm the huge, barred gate.

At that moment, two men trot into the cobble stoned square, and rein in their horses. The older of the two dismounts, and strolls over to where the priest and his men stand. They do not know the man, but there is an angry murmur, as the younger fellow, John Beckshaw, is recognised.

"Traitor!" Someone shouts from the back of the crowd, and they move forward, menacingly. The young man raises the pistol, and points it at the mob.

"Who will be first to die?" he asks, keeping his voice as calm as he can. The crowd of men stop advancing, and look to each other. The first man to go for John Beckshaw will have to take a lead ball for his trouble, and none wish to be the first martyr in the great rebellion.

"You do well to listen to my young friend," Will Draper shouts. "For my troop of King's Horse is but a couple of miles behind. Before nightfall, your town will be in flames, and most of you will be hanging, next to this … *Irish* priest. Now, name yourself, scoundrel!"

"I am Father Dominic O'Hanlon," the priest snarls. "I am the appointed representative of His Grace, Pope Clement."

"And I am Colonel Will Draper, the King's Examiner, come to scourge papists from his realm. You are under arrest, Master Priest."

"Kill him!" The priest is mad with rage, and affronted that a mere soldier defies his master, in Rome. The crowd makes a forward move, and Father Dominic hefts, one handed, his huge, double edged axe.

John Beckshaw forgets his instructions, and closes both eyes as he fires. The pistol's lead shot hit's the nearest man in the foot, and he screams in pain. The priest raises his axe, and Will, with surprising speed, draws his German forged sword, and delivers a savage back handed blow. There is a gasp from the crowd, as Father Dominic's severed head bounces on the cobbles. For a moment, the giant body stands, headless, then crumples to the ground.

"God save King Henry!" Joshua Beckshaw shouts, and a dozen men rush forward, waving makeshift weapons, and crying their support for the king. The stunned, once rebellious, crowd parts, leaving three of their number shaking with fear. It is over in minutes, and the great Skipton rebellion is nipped in the bud.

"Take them away," Joshua Beckshaw orders, and the three men are bound, and dragged off. "I have never before seen such a thing, sir!"

"Had he posted guards, the town would have fallen to him," Will says. "It was my good fortune that he was no soldier. Though he died bravely enough."

"Skipton is for the king, Colonel Draper," John Beckshaw says, handing back the borrowed pistol. "Now I must apologise to Master Brough, for I fear I have shot off his big toe. I shall explain that I was aiming at his heart!"

Will Draper has something to report to the king, at last. He will explain that Father Dominic was spreading sedition, but that he had no takers, save the three merchants, whom sought to profit from a rebellion, and whom he cannot save from justice. Joshua Beckshaw is the local magistrate, and will have them tried, sentenced, and hanged before the next dawn.

"Do not forget to put the heads up on the castle tower, sir," he advises, as he remounts Moll. "It will prove Skipton's loyalty to the king."

"Then your task is complete?" John Beckshaw asks.

"It is."

"I have a mind to visit London, Colonel

Draper," the young man says. "Might I ride with you?"

"What will your father say?"

"He will give me some advice, and a purse of silver. I will take the latter, and not the former. I seek adventure."

"Very well. If your father agrees, you may come with me." Will has a rush of blood to his head. "I might even offer you a place under me, as an assistant King's Examiner. How does twenty four pounds a year sound?"

"Sir, I will do it for nothing, if you but ask," John replies, happily. "Though an advance of pay might help me buy a decent sword and pistol."

"They come with the position," Will says, "as does the possibility of death at every turn."

"I care not."

"No? Then you must learn to fire a pistol, sir, for I cannot have you shooting off gentlemen's toes in error!"

*

"Did you hear?" The king is waving a report about, and striding up, and down, the throne room in a most agitated way.

"Hear what, sire?" Thomas Cromwell asks. George Boleyn and his father are present, as always, these days. They court the king, and seek to separate him from the rest of the world, at every turn.

"Rebels in Yorkshire," Henry replies, handing over the report. Cromwell has already read it, of course, but the king does not know that.

All important documents go through the Privy Councillor's hands before reaching the king.

"Goodness," he says, affecting horror. "I see that Colonel Draper has rooted them all out for you, sire."

"By God, it was a happy day when I appointed that fellow to his post," Henry says. "He has ridden the length, and the breadth of my northern lands, and destroyed my enemies. Why could not Harry Percy do that for me? The duke is a slack jawed coxcomb. Why, I have a mind to strip him of his titles."

"Sire, Lord Percy is along the borders, with the Earl of Cumberland, and ten thousand troops," Cromwell explains. "Now is not a good time to punish him. Let us wait until he has thrashed the Scots for you, then consider how to proceed."

"Well said, Thomas," Henry says, calming down. "How do I reward the good colonel?"

"He is rewarded enough, sire," George Boleyn says. "The man is of Irish birth, I hear, and that is as low as can be. Do not honour him above his station in life any further, sire."

"Just so," the father puts in. "Nor does he need a money reward. It is rumoured that he is richer than any man in your realm."

"What is this?" Henry admires self made men, but he does not like them to be too good at what they do.

"The fellow earns a hundred a year, sire," Thomas Cromwell puts in, hurriedly. "His wife, Mistress Miriam, has a successful mercantile business, and pays her taxes in full, and on time. Unlike some I could name."

"Do you look at me, sir?" *Monsignour* demands.

"I simply look," Cromwell says. "There are those who think the treasury fills itself. If you wish to reward so loyal a man, sire, then give him a pay rise. With two hundred a year, he can train others in his methods, who will serve you just as well. Your Majesty will be the only royalty in the whole world with his own private Examiner's Office. The emperor will be livid, and poor, gibbering François will fall off his throne in envy."

"A splendid idea. See to it, Thomas. Now, what of the queen? I have been forbidden her company for some days."

"My daughter, the Queen of England, is quite near her time, cousin," the older Boleyn says. He has taken to calling Henry 'cousin' at every opportunity, not realising how it annoys the king, who dislikes too much familiarity, even from his father-in-law, and his family. "It is best that she remain in close confinement, until your son is born."

"Very well. I suppose I must make my own entertainment then," the king tells them. "Let us have a joust, George. I have not had a good joust since …"

"Since poor Charles Brandon struck such an unlucky blow, sire," Cromwell tells his king. "We thought you dead. Perhaps you might prefer a day hawking, or we could have my son bring his new greyhounds for you to examine?"

"You have a son, Thomas?" Henry often forgets the niceties of those who serve him, and does not recall Cromwell even being married.

"Not a bastard, is he?"

"No, sire. Gregory's mother died, some years ago."

"Ah, yes. I recall it now. Did not your daughter die also?"

"Both, sire."

"A pity. But the boy … Gregory … is well?"

"A fine young man, sire. I hope to present him at court next year. If Your Majesty permits."

"Permits? I positively *demand* it, Thomas." The king suddenly throws his head back, and roars laughing at a sudden thought. "Why, he can join me in our joust, Thomas. Have him suited out in armour, and I will try him out."

"Sire, he is my only son," Cromwell says, somewhat alarmed. "The boy cannot stand up to such a man as you."

"Bosh, I will treat him kindly, old friend. Now, let us make plans, for I am growing bored!"

*

"Father, the king wants me to joust against him," Gregory says, almost falling over with excitement. "Can there be a greater honour in all the wide world?"

"Gregory, my son," Cromwell replies. "The king's armourer has a suit small enough for you, and will hire it to me for twenty pounds. The sword, mace, and gauntlets, I must buy, for another forty three pounds. Your day's fun will cost me the best part of a hundred pounds!"

"It will come back ten fold, when I am accepted at court, father," Gregory replies, happily.

"Any post, working with the king, will bring me in easily that much, each year."

"You are not yet fourteen," Cromwell says. "Any of the gentlemen who joust today, could cut you down in a moment."

"Oh, I will take my knocks, and give back more," Gregory tells his father. Though he has his mother's fine looks, he lacks Cromwell's brains, and is destined to be little more than an entertaining courtier.

"Not to the king," Cromwell says. "Whatever you do, do not strike His Majesty. Ten years ago, Charles Brandon ran a lance into the king's visor, and almost killed him. Lord Suffolk was distraught, and swore never to joust against Henry again. The king forgave him, saying that it was his own fault, for not putting down his visor."

"These things happen, father."

"Then about a year ago, Brandon landed an unlucky blow to Henry's head, and he almost died. He was addled for days, and the doctors feared his brain fever might claim his life. Charles Brandon is the king's best friend, but he escaped being killed by the king's men, only because I intervened."

"That was bad luck."

"Yes, imagine then if some grandson of a blacksmith hurt the king?" Cromwell raises a finger, and runs it across his throat. We are, despite our wealth and power, peasants, my son, and that means we do not get royal pardons. So, if the king comes at you, let him tap you, and fall down. Understood?"

"But I could easily... ouch!"

"That is the first time I have ever slapped you, boy … let it be the last. Now, do as I tell you!"

*

"The king is holding an impromptu melee," Will Draper tells his wife. "I am back but a day, and he wishes me to play with him."

"Then play. The king thinks to honour you, Will," Miriam says.

"He wishes to test my prowess."

"No, you must not fight him." Miriam knows her husband's mind. He is not one to back down, even from the king. "Find some lesser noble to thrash."

"It is just a mummery, my love," Will says. "These lords, and fine gentlemen wave their swords about, and shout silly things, just to make the ladies swoon."

"Then let them swoon, but not over you," Miriam replies, with a stern look. "I want you jousting with me this night!"

*

"Master Armourer, a word with you?" George Boleyn drops a bag of silver onto the oak table, where various swords and pieces of armour are laid out. "I would play a jest on my friend today, and seek your help."

"How so, My Lord?"

"The mêlée is a noisy, confused fight, is it not?"

"It is."

"Yet the king always ends up fighting his friend?"

"The Duke of Suffolk is the best jouster in Europe, sir," the armourer replies. "It is only fitting that they should meet. Though in all their fights, I have only ever known the king lose twice. Once when he forgot to lower his visor, and last year, when Suffolk landed a lucky blow."

"Then the king is good?"

"One of the best I have ever trained, with a sword, and a master with the lance."

"My friend boasts that he can thrash both of them."

"Does he now?" The armourer shakes his head, and smiles in disbelief. "Who is this fool?"

"Colonel Draper."

"I know of the fellow," the armourer replies. "He has a reputation for fighting bare arsed, badly armed, Irish rebels, does he not?"

"He does, and thinks it makes him a champion," Boleyn sniggers. "It might be fun to see the fellow shown up. Can it be done?"

"It depends on how I order the battles," the man explains. "If I line them up in the right way, the king always meets Suffolk at the last. If I alter the starting positions, this Draper will have to meet either Suffolk, or the king. Either one will soon knock the shit out of him, Your Lordship."

"Then let it be so," Boleyn tells the armourer. "Another purse when the fellow is grovelling under Henry's sword."

"My pleasure, My Lord. You are absolutely sure… are you not …. that the fellow will lose? If he bests the king …"

"Worry not," George Boleyn says, smirking at the thought. "Colonel Will Draper is fit only for killing Irishmen, and murdering priests."

"Sweet Christ, he killed a man of God?" The armourer forgets he is of the new faith, and fervently crosses himself. It is common knowledge that it is bad luck to kill a priest, and the man wonders what possessed this Draper fellow to do such a thing.

"Cut his damned head clean off," George Boleyn replies, allowing his wicked spite full reign. "Whilst this priest fellow's back was turned, I hear!"

"Then he is already cursed," the armourer says, knowingly. "The one thing you must never do, is kill a priest. No good ever comes of it!"

"Amen," George says, with a sanctimonious nod of the head. He forgets that he has been helping to close down the Roman church in England, and has countenanced many such deaths. As these royally approved murders are not by his own hand, he does not count them as sins in the eyes of God.

"Proper bad luck, that."

"Then you will arrange matters?"

"Why not?" the armourer says. "Why, 'tis only a jest, and the money will come in handy. The wife wants a new thatch for the cottage. She has her eye on that expensive Suffolk reed. Bloody woman thinks I make my own gold!"

"What?" George is struck by the casual remark. "Make your own gold? What do you know of that?"

"Know?" the man asks. "Why that pigs cannot fly, hags curdle milk, and you cannot spin gold from straw. What is there to know, sir? Why, I doubt even that new magician can make gold."

"Mercurius?"

"Yes, the one who has vanished."

"Yes, the king was most disappointed at not meeting him," George Boleyn replies. "Vanished, you say?"

"Poof!" The man waves his hands about, and chuckles. "I expect he has taken himself off to Yorkshire, where they are damned fool enough to admire his heathen tricks."

"I expect so," George Boleyn concludes. "Let us enjoy our little jest, this day, Master Armourer, and I shall drop off another bag of coins, after Colonel Draper is brought low, and made to know his place."

"That's the trouble with young folk, these days," the man agrees. "Not enough of us, knows our places. Why, in my day, a gentleman like you would have sent a servant to do his dirty work. I do not say you are at fault, sir, but it does encourage over familiarity."

7   The Tournament

"Who is in the List, Charles?" Henry is being suited up, piece by piece, into the most splendid armour ever made. The Italian designed equipment has cost him almost a thousand pounds, and it fits him to perfection.

"The usual," Brandon replies, fiddling with one of his gauntlets. "Harry Norris of course, though he is as knock kneed as can be. Then there is Cromwell's boy. He is a plucky lad. Only thirteen, I believe."

"We must give him quarter, and not beat him about too much, Charles."

"Yes sire."

"Who else?"

"Crompton, Darcy, Wyatt, the Boleyns, Sir Roderick Travis, Master Rich, who has found enough to buy armour, and another few, who wish to try their hand against the best."

"Travis, do I know the fellow?"

"The privateer, Hal. He is to be your new admiral. Cromwell recommended him. You must remember, when poor Martell ended up dead. That was an odd business."

"It was Cromwell's to sort out," Henry says, carefully. He does not want his dark secret to come out, and looking into Martell's murder again, might just upset things. "What about Colonel Will Draper, Charles ... we simply must have Draper. Let us see how the fellow stands up to some real fighting. Did you hear this latest rumour, about him murdering a priest?"

"Stuff and nonsense, Hal," the Duke of

Suffolk says. "He killed the fellow in a fair fight. For 'twas an Irishman, intent on rebellion. He was as priestly as my arse ... which is the only part of me with which I address the Bishop of Rome."

"Ha! Your wit is priceless, my dear old friend," Henry has an image in his mind of Brandon, flatulating at Pope Clement, in Rome. "Then my King's Examiner is beyond reproach?"

"Without a doubt, dear Hal," Suffolk insists. "This silly story comes from one who dislikes him, and envies his success."

"Do we know whom misuses my man in so foul a manner?"

"We do, but we do not speak of such things ... lest your wife becomes upset."

"Oh, I see." Henry frowns. "George Boleyn is a shifty little bastard, as is his father, but I cannot upset the queen."

"Quite so, sire. Oh, I almost forgot ... Uncle Norfolk is also taking the field. I tried to dissuade him, but he has a young mistress to impress."

"She is well worth impressing, Charles," Henry says with a dirty wink. "Why, her baubies almost jump out at you. If only the Boleyn men would let me have a moments freedom, I would like to swive the girl. I hear she is willing."

"More than, Hal. More than."

"You dog ... have you? Now, tell me true."

"Not I, my friend. I cannot think of any other women, not with my dear wife ... your sister ... so close to ..." Suffolk forces a tear to come, and Henry slaps him on the back.

"Damn it all, Charles, but you have been a better husband than I thought you would. Dear

Mary would not begrudge you a few hours in another's arms. A man must have ... relief."

"I understand," Suffolk tells his friend. "Even a king must seek his manly desires, lest his health suffers. You must not let that happen, Hal, for the sake of England."

"You are right. I was thinking of bringing Mary Boleyn back to court."

"That might be unwise, at the moment," says Brandon. "It would be better to bed another. Some well respected, married lady, whose husband does not give her enough attention."

"Is there such a one?"

"Well, I am told, by the lady herself, that her husband has not swived her for these last three years, and she respects Your Majesty, ever so much."

"Really?" Henry tries to think who it might be. "Is she known to me?"

"Related."

"What? How so?" The king is intrigued.

"She is your sister-in-law."

"George's wife?" Henry strokes his beard, and smiles. "Are you sure she would…?"

"Like a rabbit, sire," Suffolk says, and they both laugh.

"Send her to me, tonight," the king says. "I will give young George's filly a gallop, and turn her into a mare."

"She will be pleased," Suffolk tells the king. "She itches to make up for lost time."

"Then we shall compare notes, afterwards," Henry declares. "For I cannot believe that you have not been in the lady's saddle."

"Once or twice," Suffolk admits. "Though she is still as sweet as a virgin. I wager she is a better swive than Norfolk's trollop."

"Norfolk... yes, he is not the man he once was."

"The silly old fool will end up getting battered again."

"Put him next to me, Charles," Henry decides. "It will keep the worst of the blows off him."

"Then let us get to it, Hal, for I seem to recall besting you last time ... even though it was a lucky blow." It is always a lucky blow, Brandon thinks. What he would give to show the king his true talent, and buff His Majesty black and blue. What he would give for a real fight, with any man worthy enough.

*

"I could not get you out of it, Will," Cromwell says. "I am sorry. These toy soldiers do not know what it is to fight."

"Then I shall show them," Will Draper says, solemnly.

"If you come upon Gregory, treat him lightly, I beg, and if he is being beaten down, too harshly, try and protect him."

"You do not need to ask, Master Cromwell," Will Draper replies. "I would sooner cut off my own arm, than hurt any of your family. I owe you so much, and wish we could be ..."

"What, Will?"

"Like it is with you, and Digby Waller."

"No, my friend. Our friendship will never be like how I am with Digby," Cromwell replies. "You will understand, one day."

"Then let me get to it. This armour is borrowed, and I must return it in a fit state. I shall defeat any who come at me."

"Bar the king," Cromwell says, then feels a cold clutch at his heart. "Dear Christ, Will... not the king. It will be your ruin!"

"I have never flinched from a fight, Master Cromwell," Will Draper tells his old friend. "Nor have I ever lost."

"Please, Will... for Miriam's sake."

"I fight, or I stand down," Will says. "If I stand down, the king will scorn me, and I will be ruined. If I fight, I shall fight to my best ability."

*

The Master of Arms moves back and forth, arranging the twenty main combatants, into their rightful places. Certain knights hold grudges, and are faced off with one another, whilst others are of too low a rank to fight a lord, and are paired against those of similar rank. The force is filled out with any servants who can wave a cudgel, and take a thumping, for a few coins.

Only by disposing of your equals, can you hope to face a man of greater stature. Defeat him, and your honour is much enhanced. On rare occasions, a young buck has fought his way into a confrontation with a younger Norfolk, or a Suffolk in his prime, and been thrashed for their trouble. It is much safer to avoid doing too well, lest you find yourself against the king.

To do so puts you at a disadvantage, for you must make a show, yet fail to land a blow, whilst Henry will belabour you until your bones break, then congratulate you for your bravery, and send along a bag of gold, to pay the doctor's fees.

Today, the well bribed armourer places Will Draper amongst the lowest of the low, who must contend with a bevy of servants, decked out with spears, clubs, and shields, whose job it is to provide numbers, before they can engage in single combat. To be treated so is bordering on being a mortal insult to a trained soldier.

Will is about to grab the fellow, and force him to move him forward in rank, when he sees that young Gregory has also been placed by his side. He taps the boy on the helmet, and signals for him to raise his visor.

"Keep it up, boy, until we are clear of this rabble," he advises Thomas Cromwell's only child. "Once we come up against armoured men, close it, and keep close by my side. I intend going for Suffolk, or the king, and we may win through, together."

"You honour me, Master Will," Gregory says. "Now I am here, I am shaking like a leaf."

"I am afraid too," Will tells him. "Only a fool actually likes to fight, and they seldom live long. Remember what you have been taught. Do not overreach, Keep your shield up, and guard your left flank. Ready?"

"Yes, I think so."

"Remember how you rode through those rogues who sought to kidnap the old queen?" Will says, bolstering the boy's courage.

"By God, yes, I did, did I not? They scattered to the winds before me."

"Quite." Will Draper smiles, and watches for the tournament pennant to be waved. He turns to the nearest badly armed servant, and grins an evil grin. "By God," he says, almost conversationally, "my friend and I intend cutting all those who stand in our way to pieces. No quarter, and to the death!"

"Oh, shit!" The man, normally a fetcher of wood, and setter of fires steps away, and mutters to the man beside him. As the pennant is waved, the rabble, forewarned of the danger, part on either side of Will and Gregory.

"Charge!" Will cries, and they rush forward, towards a phalanx of startled men in armour. "Visor down, and stand fast, boy!"

Almost at once, Crompton, an old friend of Henry's approaches, as if to pass the time of day. Will does not slow down, but rushes inside the man's lazy swing of the sword, and shoulder charges him, using his shield like a battering ram. The man grunts, and topples backwards under the onslaught. Will strides over him, and delivers two solid whacks with his blunted sword to Sir Roderick Travis' shield. Henry's newest Admiral of the Fleet staggers back a pace or two, and curses.

"By God, Will, but you mean business," he curses, and tries a backhanded cut, which Will flicks aside, before delivering a crashing blow to the mans helmet. Travis staggers away, with his head ringing from the hit. He has the good sense to hold up his hand, as a sign that he begs for quarter.

Will turns from the defeated man, and pushes on, with young Gregory shielding his left flank.

Then, suddenly, amidst the general mayhem, Charles Brandon, Duke of Suffolk, and best jouster in Europe, stands before him. He is as tall, and broader than Will, and he has the better armour, and weaponry.

"What ho, Will!" he says, cheerfully. He sets his feet apart, ready to withstand any sudden rush. "You have done well… but now…" He lunges, and Will Draper takes the blow on his shield. And is forced to give ground, if only a step.

*

Gregory's ill fitting visor almost makes him blind, and he contents himself with following Will, and lashing left and right at any who venture too close. Men are fighting all around, settling old scores, or creating new grudges. It seems that no one is interested in jousting with a mere boy.

Then, to one side, a voice rings out a challenge. Gregory turns, and is met by the most amazing sight. A knight, no taller than he, dressed in French armour, and bedecked with the most amazing feathers in his helmet, offers to fight. Gregory swings his blunted sword, and the little man dances away, and parries. Then he dances back and delivers a light blow to Gregory's armoured shoulder.

The boy winces, and slashes back. His little opponent leaps back, and lures Gregory further away from the main mêlée, as if keeping him from Will's side. Gregory rushes forward, with shield raised, and chops down at the man's wrist. The fellow pulls back from the blow, but Gregory's blade catches the man's sword, and knocks it from his gauntleted hand.

"Quarter, good sir," the man cries, and throws open his visor.

"Master Chapuys?" Gregory Cromwell is surprised, and a little confused.

"You have defeated me in your first joust, Gregory, and I salute you. Now, come from the field for your father's sake!"

"Be damned if I shall," Gregory cries, as he realises that his father has set up this duel. He turns to look for Will, whose flank he is sworn to guard.

*

Charles Brandon has no wish to humiliate Will Draper, and decides to disarm him quickly. He employs is favourite feint, crossing his sword back and forth, before delivering a blunted thrust, that would kill under normal battle conditions. In twenty years, it has never failed him.

His sword point meets empty air, and he has just enough time to realise that Draper has gone, before the flat of a sword blade clangs against his helmet. He curses, and tries to regain the upper hand, but Will is already inside his guard, battering him down with blow after blow. He has no choice but to raise his arm, and yield.

"By God, but I have a new champion!" Henry shouts, and roars with laughter. "Stay down, Charles, whilst I deal with Colonel Draper!"

The king comes on, and beats at Will's upraised shield, only to receive a blow in return that dents his own. Henry grunts and pushes forward, knowing that his greater height, and extra weight, will overcome Will's resistance. The King's Examiner pushes back, and the two look eye to eye through their visors slits. It is a battle of wills, as well as strength.

Will senses that he has the edge over the king, and that he is younger and fitter. It will be an easy matter to turn his man, and deliver a sharp blow to the king's back. He cannot resist, and knows he cannot fail. It is against his nature to let any man best him… even a king.

*

Gregory sees Brandon go down onto his knees, and Will holding off the king's first mad lunge. He gives a great yell, raises his shield, and charges the king. Suffolk, having yielded, staggers to his feet, across Gregory's path, and takes the full brunt of the charge. The impact sends him reeling, into the exposed back of Will Draper, who is thrust sideways.

Will falls to one knee, and the king is on him, pressing his blunt blade against his throat. For one , mad moment, Will considers drawing the knife from his belt, and feinting under Henry's blade. It is a battlefield move, and he has killed many men with it.

"Yield, sir!" Henry demands. "For pity's sake, yield with honour, for I know when I am well matched."

Will nods his head, and the blade is removed. Henry holds out a gloved hand, and helps him to his feet. Brandon is recovered, and is pulling Gregory back into a standing position.

"By God, Harry, but these two fellows almost had us that time," Suffolk says, adopting the voice he always uses to curry favour with his childhood friend. "I swear they had a plan, and plotted to bring us *both* down. Thank God, you held firm, for I was sitting on my arse."

"Yes, you were, old friend. Leaving me to deal with these two rogues at once!" Henry is already beginning to believe his own fiction. "I swear you are a man after my own heart, Colonel Draper."

"Your Majesty flatters me."

"I *never* flatter," Henry says. "There is no need, for I am the king. My compliment is well said, and well meant, sir. Now, who is your dwarf-like friend?"

"Master Gregory Cromwell, Your Highness," Suffolk says, effecting a royal introduction. "The fruit does not fall far from the tree. The lad shows great promise … if only he stops falling over his betters."

"Ha! Just so, Charles," Henry is in an expansive mood. He sees that the household servants are getting their usual battering, and calls a halt to the mêlée. "Do we have any casualties? Go and see, Charles. Make sure the doctors are on hand, and give the servants a few extra coppers for their bruises."

"At once, sire," Suffolk says, and goes off on his errand.

"Well, I am for a glass of wine," Henry says. "Draper, you and the boy, must join me in my pavilion, once you have taken off that awful armour. Did you see that bantam cock, with the huge feathers in his helmet?"

"Ambassador Chapuys, sire," Gregory admits. "I fear I gave him a terrible whack, when I disarmed him."

"An *arm-bassador* without arms, "Henry says, and goes off, laughing at his own jest.

"That was prettily done, Colonel Draper." Will turns, to find Norfolk standing to one side. He is no man's fool, and has dodged most of the fighting. No one would dare injure the Duke of Norfolk, and he has spent a few minutes, clouting a couple of servants, and kicking Crompton, whilst he was still down on the ground. "Would you really have used that knife?"

"Sir?" Will shows no emotion at being caught out.

"I saw it in your stance," Norfolk continues. "Had it not been Henry, you would have gutted your man, would you not?"

"I did not learn to fight in a pretty way, My Lord Norfolk," he says. "In Ireland, men will drop from trees, or leap out of bushes, and cut your throat, before you can cry for help. You learn to kill, in what ever way you can."

"Once, when I was young, I strangled a fellow with my bare hands," Norfolk says, as if discoursing in polite society. "The Scots had sneaked into our camp, and almost took us unawares. I was unarmed, and did as you have said. I killed, with what I had at my disposal. Lord, but how the bastard's eyes bulged."

"It is not an easy death." Will wonders why he is being told the story. "I take it that you drove the attack off?"

"We lost three men, but killed a dozen of them. I had their heads lopped off, and stuck on spikes." Norfolk smiles benignly. "One day. Your old master and I will clash. You would do well to be on the right side by then."

"Thank you for your concern, My Lord," Will says, and sets off towards the tents.

"The old bastard," Gregory says. "He would buy you, if he could, Will."

"That he will never do. Mark his words well though, Gregory. One day, you may have to kill the man, to save your father. Is that something you could do?"

"Without a moment's pause," Gregory says. "And I will do that bastard George Boleyn too, for doing this to you."

"What has George Boleyn got to do with it?" Will asks, then realises why he was insulted, and why he was set up to fight the king. "You know this?"

"Yes, the royal armourer was bribed to arrange matters," Gregory explains. "Once he had been paid, he came to father, and told him what George had done. He is on our strength, you see."

"Then George must pay."

"He is on his way to get out of his armour," Gregory observes. "If we cut across the field, we can head him off."

Will steps up his pace, and comes on Boleyn just as he reaches the tent's opening. The ground underfoot is churned into a muddied mess by a hundred armoured feet.

"George!" Boleyn turns, and almost gags in fear, as he sees Will Draper coming at him. He tries to run, but stumbles, and goes face down into the thick mud. Will places a heavy foot on the fallen man's helmet, and pushes down. The younger Boleyn's arms and legs begin to wave about, as the mud fills his visor, and clogs his mouth and nose.

"Hold, sir!" A page comes running over, and is soon joined by more of Boleyn's men. Will removes his foot, and allows them to haul their master up onto his feet. He waits until they drag off his helmet, and allow him to gasp in some air, before, quite deliberately, smacking his face.

"At your service, *My Lord*, anytime you wish." Will says. "I would settle our quarrel know, except the king demands my presence. He is much taken with Gregory and myself, it seems. Good day to you."

"I wager he was scared," Gregory says, excitedly, as the return to their own tents. "The fool must have really believed you would have killed him."

"I would have, had not his men come," Will Draper replies, grimly. "One day, the house of Cromwell, and the house of Boleyn must clash, and I will have to kill him anyway."

"Then I will be by your side," Gregory says.

"Rather that than under my feet," Will replies, and they both laugh. For the moment, Henry likes them, and they must take full advantage of his friendship. The queen is close to giving birth, and such an event can only make the Boleyns' stronger.

An England ruled by the Boleyn clan is not a pretty thing to consider, and Will hopes, as does everyone at Austin Friars, that it never comes about.

8   The King's Magician

"Your Majesty honours my family," Thomas Cromwell says, as the king is divested of his expensive armour. "Your acknowledgement of my son, Gregory was most gracious."

"Bugger me, Thomas, the lad bettered that damned Imperial Ambassador, Chapuys," Henry tells his minister. "The little French bastard. What is he doing working for the Emperor Charles, anyway?"

"He is a Savoyard, sire, not a Frenchman."

"He speaks French."

"And Latin, German, Italian, Flemish, and English, sire," Cromwell explains. "He has been most helpful in the matter of the divorce."

"Has he?"

"Yes, sire. M'sieu Chapuys kept Clement in an obstinate mood, and helped us bring the Venetians out against any annulment. Because of that we were able to bring in our new laws, and force through a divorce."

"I see. We should reward him then."

"Your Highness has already signed the papers, awarding Chapuys a small pension. He will receive a hundred a year, once he has left the employ of the Holy Roman Empire."

"You are a clever fellow, Thomas," Henry concludes. "Will you join us for dinner. Nothing as grand as your table, but a goodly spread, I wager."

"I regret, sire, that state business keeps me from my dinner tonight," Cromwell says, apologetically. "It seems that there are some irregularities with the royal treasury."

"Irregularities?" Henry asks.

"Nothing to worry about, sire," Cromwell explains. "Some careless clerk has placed a nought in the wrong column, and the figures do not match. It seems that there was no church revenue, these last three months."

"But that cannot be," the king says.

"No, it cannot. I will find the error, and give Your Majesty a full report, when next we meet.

"All will be well with you in charge, old friend," the king tells Cromwell. "You are a magician with figures."

"Then perhaps you might appoint me as the King's Magician," Cromwell jests.

"And have them burn you at the stake?" Henry replies, smiling. "I think not, Tom. I think not. Now, be off, and I will make do with lesser company."

*

"Lady Jane Rochford, Your Highness," Suffolk says, introducing George Boleyn's misused wife to the king. He squints at her over his goblet, and smiles. At twenty seven, the woman is in her prime, and is prettier than most at court.

"Ah, yes. Georges wife. I seem to recall you about the court, my dear girl. Do you wait on the queen?"

"I do, sire." Lady Jane has been warned by Suffolk that the king is in an amorous mood, and what she can expect. Once he has bedded a lady, Henry can be most generous. "Though we have never been formally introduced. My idiot of a husband has been most remiss. Perhaps he fears me meeting a *real* man."

"Come and sit with me, child," the king says, and pats the seat by his side. "Let a real man whisper in your ear."

"Your Majesty," Will Draper bows, and pushes Gregory into a vacant seat at the foot of the table.

"Will, come here, and sit beside me. Piss off now, Crompton, your pathetic jests begin to weary me." Crompton, a long standing friend, smiles, and bows himself away, and down the table, where he glowers at the usurper who takes his place.

"You almost had me today," Henry says. "I must be getting too old."

"Is the oak merely old, sire, or does it gain in strength as it ages?" Henry turns to see who has interrupted him so eloquently.

"Ah, Tom Wyatt, you cunning bastard. What hole have you crawled out of?"

"I have recently been out of town, sire," Wyatt replies, sitting next but one, down from Will, where *Monsignour* should be. "I have come into funds again, and so have returned. It is my good fortune that, whilst away, two of my creditors have died; one of the purple pox, and the other of old age. You were wonderful in the mêlée, sire."

"I was, was I not?" Henry drinks off his goblet of wine, and grips Lady Jane's plump little thigh with his free hand. "Eat up quickly, lads, for I am tired, and will soon need my bed." He leers at George's wife, and she simpers back at him.

"I am driven by my muse, Your Majesty, to

compose an ode to honour the event. Might I employ your bravery within my poetic scrawling?"

"Scrawling? You are our finest poet, Wyatt, as well you know." Henry gives praise, in order to receive more back.

"The finest, sire?" Wyatt shakes his head. "Then why, wherever I travel, they play another's airs instead of mine? No, I confess I am brilliant, but you outshine me. Your words, when set to music have a certain ... effect, that mine does not."

"I confess that my music is admired," Henry says, "but one never knows if it is flattery, because I am king."

"Sire, in Norwich, and York, they dance to your tunes, without knowing if they be by a king, or a commoner. Only my dirtier poems are ever repeated."

" No wonder, for I have never met a randier fellow," the king declares.

"Save only Your Majesty," Will says, and they all laugh.

"My chair, I do believe, sir." *Monsignour* is affronted that someone is actually in his seat.

"My arse, I believe sir," Tom Wyatt replies.

"Your Majesty, this is too much." The older Boleyn turns to Henry for assistance. His lip is curled, most petulantly, and he is shaking with anger.

"Oh, let him sit down, Wyatt." Henry does not want to upset his wife's father, so close to the birth of his child, yet dislikes having to pander to his churlish ways, and perceived slights.

"With the greatest of pleasure, sire, for the

chair does smell of ... old farts!" The poet stands, and gestures for Boleyn to be seated. Henry is stifling a guffaw, for he has a weakness for childish humour, that Wyatt plays to, perfectly.

"Lady Jane, perhaps you might leave us to our manly talk. I will speak with you, anon." He leans across, and whispers into her ear. "You know where my bedroom is, do you not?"

"I look forward to seeing your mighty oak, sire," she mutters back, and he grins like a small schoolboy.

"Where is that boy of yours, Boleyn?" the king asks.

"He is unwell, sire, and begs your pardon."

"Is it something he ate?" Will asks, and *Monsignour* sticks his nose in the air, and ignores the remark. Henry senses that there is something he has missed, and wonders at how the two men dislike one another so much. "I hope the king is not too insulted by poor George's absence."

"I see Cromwell is not here either," Boleyn snaps back.

"My royal magician is working his spells on the royal treasury," Henry says. He is slightly drunk, and does not see the look on Boleyn's face.

"Master Cromwell is too fond of courting Your Majesty's wealth."

"Why not," Will replies. "He has made most of it for the king. If not for Thomas Cromwell, and Cardinal Wolsey before him, the coffers would be empty."

"Ah, dear old Wolsey," Henry moans. "If only he had lived another day, for I was about to pardon him, and restore him to his former glory.

Have I ever mentioned that to you fellows?"

"Your Majesty is, as ever, too kind," Wyatt mutters.

"What's this, started without old Uncle Norfolk?" The duke comes in, and looks about for an empty place, not too far from the king. Will Draper stands, and offers his own chair to the duke, who waves him back down. "I will sit here, amongst theses lower class rogues. The jesting is usually cruder, and much funnier. Is that you Tom Wyatt?"

"Is that you, father?" Tom Wyatt replies. "Ah, no it is not. For I am one of the few men from Norfolk not sired by you, sir."

"You lying scoundrel," Norfolk scolds, but in a genial sort of way. He thinks back to recall if he ever had swived Wyatt's mother, but his memory is not what it once was, and his lovers run into the hundreds. "Give us a ballad, you young bugger!"

Wyatt thinks for a moment, then begins a soft, lilting air. The room falls silent, at the sound of his soft baritone voice.

> *'I shall sing a song of our Good King Harry,*
> *whose strong right arm brought Will Draper*
> *low, and turning aside his cleverest parry,*
> *The king did deal him such a mortal blow,*
>
> *Now our Hal wishes not to tarry,*
> *For his Lady Jane lies a bed,*
> *and her keep, our Hal must carry,*
> *To let his stallion have its head.'*

The room becomes tense with expectation. All heads turn to watch *Monsignour's* reaction to Tom Wyatt's song, but he acts as if he has not heard a word. The silence is broken by Henry's cackling laughter. He lurches up, and raises his goblet into the air.

"Uncle Norfolk, gentlemen, I must let my stallion roam where ever it might. Good night to you all!" He lurches from the hall, accompanied by Crompton, and several more hangers on. They will undress him, and ease him into bed beside Lady Jane, without noticing her presence. Nor will they 'see' her flitting back to her own chambers, come the morning.

Lady Jane awaits the king's attentions, for she has no other choice. It is only after a few minutes of his heavy breathing that she realises that His Majesty has fallen into a drunken stupor. It is a simple thing to wait for a suitable length of time, before slipping away. The king will never admit that he was too drunk to swive her, and she will keep the secret too.

"In the morning, your daughter-in-law will be a richer woman, *Monsignour*," Tom Wyatt says, grinning at Boleyn. "I wager Henry is her first real man."

"I will take that wager," Suffolk calls, and the room erupts into boisterous laughter. Thomas Boleyn stands, and waits for the noise to abate.

"In a few days, the king will have a new heir, and I will have my revenge on every man who now laughs at my family. I will see you kicked from your post, Draper, and have your old master dragged out of Austin Friars, and hanged like a common criminal."

"Is it something we have said, My Lord?" Norfolk growls, and the room bursts into fresh gales of laughter. Boleyn raises his nose in to the air, in what he thinks is a dignified manner, and leaves the hall. Behind him, someone makes a rude noise with their lips.

"Then Henry is tupping George's wife?" Norfolk asks. "About time. The girl must be desperate for a swive. Little George hardly seems up to the task."

"It seems to have been a bad day for the Boleyns," Suffolk says. "Let us hope that all goes well with the queen."

"Careful, Charles," Norfolk warns. "You can skin Boleyn, and his bastard son, for all I care, but do not speak ill off Anne. My niece is a bitch of the first order, but she carries the future of England in her belly."

"One can only hope," Suffolk replies. There is a commotion, and the doors to the great hall are thrown open. Mush and Richard come in, and make straight for Will. He stands to meet them, fearing that something has gone awry.

"Master Cromwell begs your presence at once, Colonel Draper," Richard says.

"Of course," Will replies. The diners watch as he and Gregory are marched from the room. Once outside, Will turns to Mush. "Well, what is it?"

"Cromwell is in trouble," Mush says.

"Is it bad?" Gregory asks.

"I think so," Mush tells them. "He seemed very happy when he came from here, earlier on, as if one of his schemes was about to bear fruit. Then a messenger came, from Folkestone, and the master locked himself away in his study. Next thing we know, he is demanding to see you, and he is in a terrible state."

"I am the king's man now," Will says. "Whatever it is, must not be against His Majesty."

"Is this the king you were going to slaughter at the tourney?" Richard says. "It is the talk of the court, how you could have killed him, but forbore."

"A stupid tale, spread by a stupid man," Will says.

"Cromwell needs you."

"What about Master Waller?" Will says, sharply. "Can he not do what must be done?"

"Digby Waller?" Mush frowns at this. "He is not yet one of us, Will. It has always been we select few who Cromwell turns to, when there is trouble. Will you let him down now?"

"Of course not," Will says. "Though he has played me false again."

"How so?"

"The alchemist."

"Ah, you know something then?" Richard says.

"I do now," Will tells him. "I just do not understand why Cromwell kept me at a distance."

"To keep you uncompromised," Mush says. "He did not want Henry to think you were still Cromwell's man. Then, when the time comes, the king will trust your word."

"I see," Will says, but he does not. Thomas Cromwell is mixed up in something again, and needs his help. That seems to be enough reason for his old master to demand his attendance.

They hurry through the deserted streets, and come to an Austin Friars ablaze with light. Every room is bedecked with candles, and torches burn about the courtyard, as if to ward off some evil thing. Will strides into the entrance hall, and stares. On the long bench outside Cromwell's study, Barnaby Fowler sits, and beside him are the alchemist, and his confederate, Popo.

"God's teeth!" Will throws off his cloak, and raps on the master's closed door.

"Who is it?"

"Will, sir." The door flies open, and he is urged to step inside by a grey faced Cromwell. "What is it?"

"Disaster," Thomas Cromwell says, slamming the door on the rest. "I have been a fool, and risked too much. Now I must pay the price."

"Because of this nonsense with your alchemist?" Will asks.

"Ah, you know then?" Cromwell looks sheepish, and pours out two glasses of red wine.

"Not at first," Will confesses. "You played it very well, and I fell for the great lie, because the small lie was so convincing. Like the rest around the table that night, I saw Mercurius actually read minds. There was no doubt about it. So, when he mentioned being able to make gold, I was ready to believe his ridiculous claim."

"You saw the *apparatus diaboli* work, did you not?"

"We all did," Will says. "As I said. The small lie led us to fall for the grand one. I actually believed the man could divine thoughts, until I realised that he had an accomplice, other than his fat friend. When the questions were written down and placed on the platter, all you had to do was make sure yours was at the bottom of the pile."

"Yes, so simple, was it not?" Cromwell asks.

"Very clever. Mercurius pretends the top question is yours, and gives a prearranged answer. You are amazed, and he opens the paper. Once he has read what is really written, he burns it, and uses the information to surprise one of us. The process goes on, until all have been answered, and the last paper he burns is your own."

"You should have seen your faces."

"Oh, yes, we fell for it." Will shakes his head in disgust. "Then the best trick of the night. Demonstrate the gold making box, and insist that we never talk of it again. Every man must have thought how to get a full sized one. Is that what you intended?"

"Yes. I wanted Thomas Boleyn to fall into the well laid trap," Cromwell says. "I used Digby Waller to help me. When Digby came to me, I resolved to bring Boleyn down, so had the boy call on George Boleyn, and offer to spy for him. George jumped at the chance, and we fed him a few pieces of information to make it look genuine. Then, I arranged for Digby to escort Mercurius back to his inn. Boleyn saw his chance, and had him arrange a meeting between Mercurius, and himself the next day."

"Clever."

"Digby reported back, and the meeting was set," Cromwell explains. "Aldo Mercurius, as you guessed, was already working for me. He and Popo tour the continent, putting on magic shows. I sent for them, and invented the famous alchemist, and his assistant. Boleyn demanded that Mercurius build him a full sized gold making box, and he agreed. He told Boleyn that it would cost seventy thousand, and that he wanted a share of the gold too."

"Monsignour is not so foolish as to hand over so much," Will says.

"That is true. He sought to be very clever, and told Mercurius to build his box, using a line of credit, guaranteed by the Boleyns. My alchemist was well prepared, and agreed the deal. He told Thomas Boleyn that the box would be built, but that it must be guaranteed in writing. The various craftsmen would extend credit, he explained, if they knew *Monsignour,* father-in-law of King Henry, guaranteed payment. Boleyn was flattered, and gave him a signed paper, made legal by the family seal."

"Then Mercurius drops from sight, and pretends he is working on his invention?" Will guesses.

"Yes, for these three months past. Boleyn kept everything secret, and saw that you were kept out of London. It seems he fears your investigative powers greatly." Cromwell sighs. "He was told the box was ready, and that it would be in Folkestone, today. All that was needed, was the seventy thousand pounds, to cover the costs of making."

"I wager he and George were dancing a jig," Will says, wryly.

"Of course. Boleyn had already embezzled

the money from the vast church revenues, as it arrived. He meant to use it to pay for the machine, and intended replacing the stolen amount, after the box was working."

"The fool."

"He fell for the big lie," Thomas Cromwell says. "Such men usually do. He detailed Digby, and a half dozen thugs, to deliver the money, and return with the wonderful apparatus. On the way there, twenty armed men - not mine - ambushed Boleyn's force, and stole the money."

"Then Boleyn is finished."

"As am I," Cromwell says. "The king will not believe my innocence in the matter. We will both be punished. I sought to show Boleyn up as a thief, and have destroyed myself in the process."

"Can you not simply replace the money from your own funds?" Will asks. Cromwell's wealth is fabled amongst those who know him.

"All my assets are in land and wool. I can raise about eight thousand, at short notice."

"Miriam and I will help."

"Your fortune is also invested," Cromwell replies. "I advised Miriam to keep her money locked in cargoes and a fleet of cogs. She also owns half of the building land along the Thames."

"Summon old Boleyn to see you tomorrow."

"What for?"

"I think I have a fair idea how we can clean up this mess," Will says, "but you must do several things to aid me. First, Mercurius and his friend must vanish, forever."

"I cannot have them killed," Cromwell says.

"I know that," Will replies. "Have them put

on a ship for France, and give them enough to keep them out of England. Tell them that if they return, I will cut their throats. That usually works. Then you must have Boleyn come here tomorrow morning, and arrange a small dinner for tomorrow night. I will give you the list of guests, so that the evening might prove profitable."

"What is it, Will?" Cromwell asks. "What do you know that I do not?"

"Why, sir, I know how not to be a fool!"

"Can you see a way out?"

"A narrow passage, Master Cromwell, but one that we might navigate safely."

"What is your aim?"

"Why, to put Boleyn in your power, and restore the treasury's lost thousands, of course."

"But how?" Cromwell demands to know.

"With magic, sir," Will says, and smiles at Cromwell's mystified look. "Is that not what all of this has been about?"

9   A Friendly Word

Thomas Boleyn is horror struck when news comes of the loss of his money. He realises that the seventy thousand is gone, and is at his wits end, when George reports that the gold making box is nothing but a fraud, and so compounds the tragedy.

"Dear Christ Alive, George, we are as good as ruined," he moans to his son. "If Cromwell finds out about our little loan, he will run to Henry, and denounce us."

"Perhaps he will not find out, father." George is an idiot when it comes to finance, and he thinks talking about money is for common folk. "The man is a rogue."

"A clever one. He deals with the great bankers of Europe, and knows how to account for every penny in the treasury." The elder Boleyn wrings his hands in anguish. "The king says he is already searching the accounts. It is only a matter of time."

A servant enters, bows, and hands over a folded note. Boleyn curses, and opens it, thinking it to be some supplicants application. He reads, and almost chokes.

"It from Cromwell. He wishes to see me, at once."

"Tell him to call on you," George snaps. "The fellow does not know his place!"

"George, just for once, stop being such a complete idiot. He knows, damn it. The fellow knows!"

"Shall I come with you?"

"No, stay here. I do not wish to antagonise

the man any further than necessary," Boleyn replies. "If I am arrested, go to Anne, and plead my case."

"Perhaps she has seventy thousand pounds to spare?" George says.

"That she can lay hands on within the next hour?" Boleyn sneers. "No wonder half the court make fun of you, and the rest bed your wife!"

"What?" George is taken aback. He knows about Suffolk, but that is a quid pro quo situation, as he is swiving his mistress in return. "Name the fellow, and I will call him out!"

"The king, you stupid dolt," Old Boleyn snaps. "Now, let me be on my way. Perhaps there is some hope, for he has not send soldiers to arrest me yet!"

*

"Shall I leave you?" Will asks. He is in Cromwell's study, and expects Thomas Boleyn, the 1st Earl of Wiltshire, to come calling at any moment.

"No, we will meet him in the great hall," Thomas Cromwell decides. He has regained his composure, and is looking forward to the day ahead. Thanks to Will Draper, there is a chance he might yet prevail. "When this is over, I promise you that I…"

"No!" Will holds up a hand to silence him. "Do not promise that you will always play me true in future, sir. For it is not in your nature, and I would not have you restricted by honesty."

"Cruelly said, but true enough," Cromwell

replies. "Let us move across to the great hall." They are no sooner in place than Richard announces that *Monsignour* Thomas Boleyn, 1st Earl of Wiltshire has come calling. "Show him in, nephew, and guard outside the door. Let no one in."

Boleyn slides into the great hall, and covers the twenty paces to where Cromwell stands, with trepidation. Out of the corner of his eye, he sees Will Draper standing by the window. He bows to Cromwell, for the first time ever.

"Master Cromwell, you wish to speak with me?"

"Ah, yes, a friendly word, sir," Cromwell says. "I have been going over the royal treasury accounts."

"I can explain."

"As can I," Thomas Cromwell tells him, coldly. "Every week, for the last three months, revenue from the closing down of Roman Catholic churches, and abbeys, has been diverted into your pocket. I assume that the king has authorised the loan?"

"I might have mentioned it to him … in passing." Boleyn is trapped, and finds himself unable to formulate a sensible answer.

"In passing, sir?" Thomas Cromwell shakes his head. "This will not do. Where is the paperwork for such a loan? Have you the king's seal on the arrangement?"

"Not exactly."

"Not at all." Cromwell corrects the dithering earl.

"Yes, not at all," Boleyn confesses, and his

eyes fill with tears. "It was meant only as a short term loan, and I did not wish to bother Henry at this time. Then something went wrong."

"Never mind, sir. You are the king's father-in-law, and the odd loan is not a problem, providing it is repaid, on demand. I fear that the king will want his money back, at once."

"I do not have it."

"Seventy two thousand pounds, and you do not have it?"

"Seventy, Master Cromwell!"

"You forget the interest, *Monsignour*."

"I see you are enjoying this, sir," Boleyn says, raising his voice. All he has left in his armoury now is bluster, and threats. "Do not meddle in Boleyn affairs."

"Of course not, My Lord," Cromwell replies. "Though strictly speaking, this is the king's affair, is it not?" Boleyn casts his eyes down, like a small lad, caught scrumping apples. "Where is the money, sir?"

"Stolen."

"By whom?"

"I know not, Cromwell. A gang of armed men waylaid the wagon, and robbed it," Thomas Boleyn confesses. "I have neither the money, nor the …"

"Nor the what?"

"Nor the gold making box."

"Ah, I see. Did I not warn everyone that we must forget the alchemist's magic box?"

"You did, of course, but …er … George convinced me that we could get it … for the king. We could have made seventy thousand back overnight."

"Had it worked."

"Yes."

"Which it does not?"

"No. It was a damnable fraud. The alchemist duped us all."

"Duped you, sir… not I. I knew he was a trickster, right from the start," Cromwell boasts.

"Then I wish you had told me!" Boleyn wishes to blame anyone, but himself.

"I did not think you were about to steal seventy three thousand pounds from King Henry, sir!" Boleyn notes that he has been charged another thousand interest, since the 'friendly word' has begun. "I thought we would all laugh, and go home. Now, what to do with you, My Lord."

"That is for Henry to decide."

"Are you completely mad?" Thomas Cromwell calls across to Will Draper. "Colonel, what will the king do, if you report this to him?"

"Strip *Monsignour,* and his brat, of all their titles, and banish them to Ireland… if he is in a good mood. Else he will have them tried for treason, and beheaded."

"Dear God, have mercy, sir!" The elder Boleyn is now in tears. "George misled me sir. He is a stupid boy, but we do not deserve the block."

"Do you have your Boleyn seal with you, sir?" Thomas Cromwell asks, and *Monsignour* takes it from the pouch hanging from his belt. "Excellent. You will draw up a paper, pledging seventy four thousand pounds to me, in respect of a personal loan to you. Your lands, and all your possessions will be put down as collateral.

Repayment will be due in two years time, and I will charge you at five percent a year."

"I do not understand." Boleyn cannot see the merit of such a deal for Cromwell, other than the extortionate interest rate demanded.

"It is simple. You owe Henry seventy thousand pounds. I will pay that amount back into the treasury tomorrow, and your life is saved. In return, you will owe me the debt. I shall expect monthly repayments, and that you keep a civil tongue in your head when we are in Henry's company."

"Is that all?" Boleyn is shaking with relief. Then a thought comes to him. "You have that much money at your disposal?"

"It has been a good year for wool," Cromwell lies. "It will almost clean me out of ready cash, but I have enough to save your fleece, Boleyn."

"I expect you want my thanks."

"No, just my money back, with interest," Cromwell says. It is an impossibility, he knows, for Boleyn's estates do not produce enough to cover the monthly payments of over three thousand.

"You will get your money, Cromwell," Boleyn snaps. "Once my grandson is heir to the throne, my revenues will rise, ten fold."

"Oh, and one more thing." Cromwell says this to the man, as he fumbles for his seal. "I am grown weary of that silly title you affect, and will call you 'Boleyn' from hence forth. You may continue to refer to me as 'Cromwell'. Now, shall we get something down in writing?"

One hour later, the loan agreement is set down in unbreakable legal language. The lawyer in Cromwell has seen that every loophole is sealed, and that any default will benefit him in land and property, to the tune of, at least, seventy four thousand pounds. Boleyn melts some wax, and presses his seal onto the document.

"A job well done," Cromwell mutters. "Now, sir, can I offer you some refreshment?"

"Will it be poisoned?"

"One never knows in Austin Friars," Cromwell replies, smiling. "Let us drink from the same flagon, if you so wish. Will, come and sup with us."

"Not I, sir," Will Draper replies. "I am sworn to revenge myself on George, and do not think it proper to drink with the father of a man I must kill one day."

"He means no real harm, Colonel Draper," Thomas Boleyn says. "He is my only son, and dear to me, despite his stupidity. If I swear to keep him away from you, will you not call him out?"

"I will try," Will says, testily. He has no intention of trailing the younger Boleyn, just to force him into a duel, but keeping the man in fear will curb his grosser offences. "Warn him that I have a fierce temper, and cannot always stay my hand. Remind him of how I slew the Irish priest, and explain that I can kill without flinching."

"I will do so, sir," Boleyn says. "Might I ask what you will tell the king about this 'friendly word'?"

"Nothing, unless he asks. Then I will say I

witnessed a loan being closed. If he asks after his treasury, I shall refer him to his Privy Councillor, Master Cromwell, who will say, truthfully, that all is well … to the last penny."

"A wise young man," Boleyn says, turning to Cromwell. "I often think that were he to have been my man, things would have ended differently. You know, I suppose, that Waller is my man?"

"I know that I sent him to you," Cromwell says.

"Ah, then I have been well and truly tricked." Boleyn makes a note to have Waller killed, at the first opportunity. Later, when things have settled back down, he will do the same to Cromwell and his followers. It is no use trying to outthink the blacksmith's son, he realises. The answer is to resort to brute force. A sudden accident at Austin Friars, or a swift knife thrust in the night, will suffice. One way or another, he will not repay one penny of Cromwell's loan.

"Come, Boleyn, no hard feelings," Cromwell says. "I forgave you for bruising my toe, the time Cardinal Wolsey had me kick your arse out of Lambeth Palace."

"You still bait me with that, sir?"

"Only to warn you. The toe has healed, and I can kick your arse again, whenever necessary!"

*

Will Draper watches Boleyn walk out of the courtyard, and smiles at the morning's events. He turns back to face Cromwell, and sees that he is not happy.

"Why the long face, Master Tom?" he asks.

"Was I too hard on him?"

"On Boleyn?" Will shakes his head. "The fellow will try and duck out of paying you back, and he will still whisper in Henry's ear, dripping his poison like a snake."

"You are right, of course. I was foolish to think I could destroy the man so easily. Though the repaying of this loan will keep him in check, for a while. Now, I have but one more problem to solve." He shivers, and holds his hands to the fire, despite it being nothing more than a few glowing embers. "The treasury is light by seventy thousand pounds, and I have assumed responsibility for the shortfall. When next in court, the king shall ask after the treasury, and I must answer him, truthfully."

"I understand," Will says. There is still more to accomplish, he thinks, and the race has not yet run its full course.

"Do you, Will. I must find seventy thousand at once, and cannot raise a tenth of that amount."

"Cheer up, sir," Will says. "Tonight we dine with a select group of friends, and I am sure we will be able to arrange matters to your satisfaction."

Cromwell thinks of who he has invited, and assesses there liquid assets. Amongst them all, they might raise fifteen thousand, which is of little use. Whatever Will has in mind, it must be done quickly, and effectively. The idea of being taken by Henry's men does not worry him, but he fears for all those whom he has succoured over the years, and who will fall with him.

"May God support your endeavour, my boy," Thomas Cromwell says. "Or all is lost."

*

"Another dinner?" Chapuys says, as he reads the invitation from Austin Friars. "Since the affair of the alchemist, Cromwell has had him to eat at least once a week, and their friendship is thriving again. "I will wear my ostrich feathers. Take them from my helmet, and arrange them on my blue cap." His servant sighs, and wonders if he will ever find a job with an English master, for this foreign gentleman is hard work.

The ambassador's armour lies, scattered about his dressing room, and bears silent testimony to his friendship with the Privy Councillor. It is years since he last wore it, and it is only out of storage now because he has done his friend a favour. Young Gregory needed a victory at the tourney, and Eustace Chapuys has provided it, at minimum cost. Neither were hurt, and the boy has been advanced in the king's eyes.

"I do hope it is the sucking pig again!"

*

"Dinner at Thomas Cromwell's place again," Charles Brandon says to his mistress. Mary, his wife, and the king's sister, has been dead for ten weeks, and he feels it is time to move on. A man cannot mourn for ever. "Boys only, I fear, my love."

"Is George Boleyn going?"

"I doubt it," Suffolk replies, testily. He still smarts from finding out that she has slept with George several times previously, but cannot complain, as he has been swiving the fellow's wife for months, and has even passed her on to the king, who says he finds her to be great fun. "It is for men, not catamites."

"Oh, I thought he was a sodomite," the girl sniggers. "Pray, sir, what is the difference?"

"Lay back, my dear, and I shall show you!"

*

"Here, my friend," Mush says, handing an invitation to Digby Weller. "Cromwell favours you. Even I do not always receive a free dinner."

"I hardly know how to behave like a gentleman," Weller admits. "These new fork devices confound me."

"Sit by me, and watch which I pick up first," Mush advises his new friend. "Though many gentlemen still prefer to take their own knives for the meat courses, and use their fingers. Always act as though you do not much care, but answer the master promptly, and honestly. Cromwell has it in mind to bring you on, Digby, and that will make your fortune."

"Then I should bring something."

"We will fetch some of Miriam's custard tarts," mush tells him. "They always go down well."

"Mistress Miriam is a wonder," Digby says, wistfully. "One day, I will have a fine house to live in, and a woman like her."

"I doubt another exists," Mush says, "At least, not this side of the world!"

*

"I have told the cook to do sucking pig again," Richard confides to Rafe Sadler. "None of that fancy stuff that the ladies love so much. A good soup, roast pig, and some sweet cake, cheese and wine will suffice, provided there is enough to feed eight."

"Nine," Rafe says, coldly. "The master has asked Digby."

"That boy is a marvel," says Richard. "He is younger than Mush, and twice as clever … though that does not say much!"

"He is a good lad," Rafe concedes. Too many good lads are coming through for his liking, and he feels that his place beside Cromwell is in some jeopardy. "Though lacking experience."

"Jealous, Rafe?"

"A little. I would like to be twenty again, and fancy free."

"Do not tell that to Mistress Ellen," Richard replies, grinning, "else she has your manhood off, with her sharp dress making shears!"

*

"Why was I not invited?" Miriam is in a mood, because Cromwell has only asked her husband to dinner. She moves in a man's world, and considers herself their equal. It is upsetting that the very man who has supported her, like a father, now sees fit to exclude her.

"It is a man's night, my dear," Will says.

"Is it now?" she snaps. "How many whores will Master Tom have in?"

"None!" Will is shocked. "You choose to misunderstand me, my love. When have I ever given you cause to doubt my complete devotion to you?"

"Never."

"Even when I was in Italy, fighting against the condottiero, and his army, I did not so much as wink at another woman."

"I know. Mush told me how chaste you were," Miriam confesses. "He would never keep something like that from me. We are blood, you see."

"I will never quite understand your sense of ... *Jewishness.*" Will enfolds her in his arms, and kisses her on her forehead. "Though I do enjoy it. Do you never miss having your own people about you?"

"We Jews must wander the world," Miriam tells him. "It is our punishment, for killing your Christ. My people have paid the price for one and a half thousand years, and will do so for as much again. We can never settle down for long."

"But we are safe enough," Will tells her. "Mush and I will protect you, and little Gwyllam, and you will make our fortune."

"Until some greedy noble whispers into the king's ear," Miriam says. "A Boleyn, or a Norfolk, who will remind the king that I, and my *blood,* are not wanted in England. They will try to take all we have from us."

"And this worries you?" Will kisses her again, but this time, on the lush red lips. He runs a hand up her spine, and she shudders with pleasure.

"No. Most of our wealth is at sea, and can be diverted to a foreign port if need be. Master Tom has our money invested in Lombard banks, and French land. I have a thousand pounds sitting in each of ten counting houses around Europe, waiting for the day the storm comes. All that remains, is for us to recognise that day, and get out of England."

"You worry too much," Will tells her. "You are married to the King's Examiner, and there are legal documents that trace your family back to Coventry, in the year Thirteen Eighty Three. You must learn to trust your adopted country."

"Queen Katherine has legal documents, proving her to be the rightful wife of the king, yet Master Thomas rewrote the law in a trice, and she is now a dispossessed woman, living in a lonely prison."

"She has over two hundred servants, a thousand acres of park land, horses, her personal jewels, and two pensions. One from King Henry, to assuage his guilt, and another from Master Cromwell, who sends her a hundred a month!"

"Oh, I did not know."

"Cromwell supports half the impoverished gentry in four counties, and funds two universities," Will concludes. "Now, the man is in a hard place, and it will take men whom he trusts, to help him. He does not invite you tonight, for fear of implicating you, if anything goes badly

badly wrong. You will be able to swear that you know nothing."

"About what?" Miriam asks.

"There, you prove my point," Will says. "You know nothing about anything. Now, I do not need to dress for another hour or so. Is there anything you can think of to pass the time?"

"Chess?"

"Oh, what a good idea," Will says, as he slips a hand into the top of her dress. "Does that not call for a lot of mating?"

*

"Are these fellows up to the task, Haskins?" George Boleyn asks of his steward. The man smiles a thin smile, and pats his bulging purse.

"For a hundred pounds, they will cut their way through Hell, My Lord," Roger Haskins tells him. "All three would have hanged, if not for your patronage. They live in your forests, and make their daily bread by robbing any passing travellers. Each man has killed before, and they are bound to you, because you own the local Sheriff, and secretly condone their actions."

"I do?" George has no idea that his steward was so cunning, and on his behalf. "Yes, I do. Need I meet them?"

"God forbid, My Lord," Haskins says, his voice registering shock. He is used to George's slowness of wit, but wonders how he has survived so long in this cruel world. "They cannot apportion any blame to you, should they be caught. If taken, the magistrate in Hever will demand they be turned over to him, for past crimes."

"Is that a good thing?"

"Sir, your family own Hever Castle," Haskins explains. "Once back in your family's jurisdiction, they know they will be allowed to quietly escape."

"I see," George Boleyn says, nodding his head. "What is a jurisdiction?"

"It means the land where you, and your father, of course, have real power."

"Ah, yes… *jurisdiction* … That's the thing, eh? Then they really are up to the task?" George asks again. The steward, who takes a slice of all Boleyn business, sighs, and explains how it will be done.

"The house is on the river front, a big, timber and brick thing. The lads will approach from upstream tonight, by rowing boat. They will be ashore, and torching the house before anyone can even wake up. They will use tarred torches, and buckets of lamp oil, to get the blaze going. Anyone inside will be caught, and burnt to a cinder, or jump to their deaths."

"I would love to watch."

"No."

"Why not?"

"This is a secret raid, to destroy Will Draper," Haskins tells his slow witted master. "If you are seen, even the king will not be able to save you. Think of it, sir… Will Draper, his wife and child, and all their servants, killed in a conflagration. The finger will point at you, and a public outcry will force Henry to act. He will want a culprit to hang."

"Oh, I see." George would like to watch his foe burn, of course, but does not wish to hang for the pleasure.

"You must dine with your father tonight, My Lord. Have some other local gentry there too. Make yourself as conspicuous as possible. Then they can testify as to your whereabouts, when your enemy dies. Your innocence will be obvious, and they must look elsewhere. After a while, they will claim it was an accident. Some careless servant who has not blown out a candle."

"That is really excellent, my dear Haskins," George Boleyn says. "My damned father tells me to hang back, and to stop upsetting Cromwell, but that is the coward's way of things. Draper is an insult to my family, and I will have him, and all those about him dead … now!"

"Yes, My Lord."

"Though it would be good if little Miriam Draper could be spared," the young Boleyn muses. "For she would make a pretty widow, and be ripe for a good swiving. I do not suppose that we could…"

"No, sir, absolutely not. They all die, and that is the end of the matter."

"Oh, very well … but I do wish I could watch!"

*

"I must dine without my husband, tonight, Megan," Miriam Draper tells her maid servant. "Master Beckshaw must provide me with company. See little Gwyllam is settled down, and I will see that all the doors, and the windows, are locked. My husband thinks me incapable of looking after myself."

"Bless him," Megan says. She enjoys working for the Drapers, for they treat her with respect, and pay her on time. Her previous master would dock her pay for the tiniest thing, and thrust his hand up her skirts whenever he pleased. Will Draper always speaks kindly to the servants, and even says 'please' when he asks for something to be done. Indeed, she reflects, the man is everything a girl might want in a fellow. Tall, handsome, rich, and kind. It is a pity, she reflects, that *he* does not want to fondle her each night. "He is such a fine man, mistress, and a good husband."

"Yes, I am lucky to have him." Miriam smiles as she remembers the delightful love making from but an hour before.

"Yes mistress," Megan says. The whole house have heard her cries of passion, and she wonders that the master has any strength left to go feasting with his friends. "I will rake out the embers, and throw them into the river. We do not want to risk a fire, do we?"

10   A Good Roast

Eustace Chapuys is pleased that the night is dry, for he does not want his splendid ostrich feathers to get wet, and go limp on him. A study of one of Thomas Cromwell's excellent books reveals to him that the ostrich bird is an amazing creature. It is almost a tall as a man, and has along neck. Its feathers are prized in Africa, and the bird is hunted by the faithless Mussulmen of the vast Ottoman Empire.

The ostrich, cannot fly, and is said to hide its head in the sand when afraid. Chapuys considers the ostrich to have a lot in common with the Boleyn family, and thanks God that they are not invited tonight. Instead, he expects a convivial evening of risqué stories, and fine wine. Cromwell keeps the best cellar in England, and is not sparing with his generosity.

*

Will Draper arrives at Austin Friars in good time, and sees Chapuys coming across the garden, from next door, which is the official embassy for the Holy Roman Empire. He waves, and smiles at the funny little man, and almost bursts out laughing when he sees the immense feathers hanging from his cap.

He does not make the mistake that, because he looks foolish, Eustace Chapuys is a fool. The man has a sharp mind, and would make a dangerous enemy, if you ever crossed him. Thomas Cromwell has invited him to make up the numbers, for real friends are few, and far between.

Will checks that his clothes are not in any disarray, as he has dallied overlong with Miriam, and ended up dressing in a hurry. He still feels excited by her looks, and the way she touches him, and wishes that he could evade this evening, and stay with her for the night. The moon is in its last quarter, and obscured by cloud, making it a cooler, darker night than of late. A night for thieves and vagabonds, he thinks. Evil likes darkness, and the streets of London will be a dangerous place tonight.

*

Richard Cromwell is annoyed to find that his linen shirt has shrunk again. The washer woman disagrees, and swears that his clothes are the same size as ever before. It is only when he goes to buckle up his belt that he accepts the truth. He must let the leather belt out another inch, to accommodate his growing girth.

"Too many good dinners, and not enough action," Rafe tells him, as he saunters into the bed chamber. "If you get any bigger, Master Tom will have to widen his doors, lest you be trapped within."

"Oh, such a merry jest," Richard growls. "I need to be in the saddle, alongside Will Draper again, hunting out our enemies. A few good scraps, and the weight will fall off me."

"The world changes," Rafe Sadler says. "There are fewer chances to pick a good fight these days. Why the last time I recall, was when that wicked Lady Norfolk caused such a ..." He trails off, as he recalls the outcome of the great fight in Suffolk, between Cromwell's men, and a band of mercenaries.

"Do not be dismayed," Richard says. "There is not a day goes by that I do not see the faces of those men, and recall how bravely they went to their deaths. A soldier should die with a sword in his hand, not kicking on a gallows. Will Draper granted them quarter, and I hanged all sixteen of them, behind his back."

"It could not be avoided."

"I know. Uncle explained, but it does not make me feel any better. Perhaps that is why I eat so much?"

"What, sorrow is making you fat now, old friend?" Rafe shakes his head, and wanders off to see if Cromwell needs any help in dressing, as his fingers are not nearly as dexterous as they once were. Age, he thinks, is a greater leveller than death.

*

Tom Wyatt is pleased to have been invited to eat at Austin Friars again. He is short of money, as usual, and a feast will raise his spirits. With luck, the meal might last until very late, and he will be able to cadge a bed for the night. Though there are several married ladies who would accommodate him, they do not provide such a good breakfast, as Cromwell does.

He has been working on a few saucy couplets, to get everyone smiling, and has a couple of pieces of court gossip which, if conversation flags, will enliven them all. It is 'common knowledge' that Queen Anne has found out about Henry swiving George Boleyn's wife, and wants her thrown out of court. Henry, quite truthfully, denies it, but there is an atmosphere' about the royal chambers.

It is also rumoured that *Monsignour* has suffered some sort of a financial reverse in his fortunes, though no one quite knows why. He was absent from court in the morning, and came back a changed man.

For the entire afternoon, he has been correcting any who address him as '*Monsignour*', saying instead that Boleyn, or Wiltshire will suffice. Wyatt wonders if he received a knock to the head at the recent joust, which has quite addled his brain. Still, he thinks, whatever the cause, it makes for a funny situation. Perhaps he might even compose something to please Thomas Cromwell, who clearly hates the fellow.

> *"Monsignour sat on a low stone wall,*
> *and Monsignour took a sudden bad fall.*
> *If only the wall be that much higher,*
> *we'd gladly build his funeral pyre."*

He chants his scurrilous little poem, improvising, even as he arrives at Austin Friars. Wyatt pauses before he enters the courtyard, and tries to pull his crumpled clothing into some sort of order. He cannot afford a valet any longer, and he is slipping into a state of personal disrepair. His chin is unshaven, but it adds to, rather than detracts from, his rugged good looks.

Wyatt is pragmatic, and takes each day as it comes, but he must confess that he is surprised that Anne Boleyn has not found a position for him, now she is queen. Instead, she employs effeminate Flemish musicians, and base flatterers, like Sir Henry Norris. He blames George for his situation, for they have never really liked one another.

As young children, Anne's brother always hated her showing any attention to other boys, and still seems inordinately jealous of his position. This attitude has made him many enemies, and Will Draper is George's current pet hate. The poet determines to warn his friend of how spiteful Boleyn can be, at the first opportunity. He would not put it past him to arrange an assassin, or inflict some other nasty revenge.

*

Cromwell is already dressed for dinner. He has chosen to deck himself out in black, from head to toe, and he looks like an executioner, looking for his hood. The black, silk trimmed, cap sits on the bed, awaiting a final decision.

Will Draper promises a surprise after dinner, and has a plan to save Austin Friars from the wrath of the king. Cromwell is in such a quandary that he accepts his young friend's word, without reservation. He is like a knight, beaten down in the mêlée, who must rise again, and fight for his very life.

"If only this damned armour of regrets, and misdeeds, were not so heavy," he muses. "Then I might move all the easier."

There is a knock at the bed chamber door, and Rafe Sadler pokes his head around. He sees how Cromwell is dressed, and frowns deeply.

"Tonight is supposed to be a meeting of good friends, master," he says. "Cannot you, perhaps, put on a clean white ruff, or a scarlet scarf, to enliven your apparel?"

"It suits my mood, Rafe," the older man replies. "I am not in the right state of mind for lace and ruffles. Besides, who will look at me, once Eustace arrives. Why, with all those feathers, one expects him to fly out of the window, at any moment."

"Ostrich birds cannot fly," Rafe tells him. "Master Chapuys never tires of telling everyone he meets. He says it is an affectation of the Mussulmen."

"I hope that there are no short sighted hunters abroad," Cromwell muses, "for he makes a pretty target."

"Shall I fetch you a bow, sir?" Rafe is gratified to see Cromwell smile at his small jest, and hopes his black humour soon lifts, for the guests are arriving. "Now, let me fetch a little colour for you."

*

Charles Brandon is in a merry mood. He has treated himself to some gold thread, and his new servant girl has embroidered the edge of his doublet with it. Always appear well off, his father used to tell him as a lad, and your creditors will believe you are good for another loan.

"Good evening, Mush," he says, striding into the entrance hall. "I have brought a couple of flasks of wine."

"Master Thomas has a cellar full, Your Lordship."

"Damn it, my friend, but you must call me Charles, in private ... or Brandon, if you wish. Are not all men equal in their cups?" Suffolk holds the wax sealed flasks up for examination. "They are a Roman vintage ... over fifty years old, and as mellow as a wench after swiving. My vintner tells me they go well with any roasted flesh."

"Then I shall have them opened at once, and given air, My Lor ... Charles." Mush goes off, smiling to himself. Suffolk is in a rare mood, and might cheer up Cromwell.

"Men only, or so I hear," Brandon says to Richard, who has just descended the stairs. He nudges the big bear of a man in his ample midriff, and winks, slyly.

"That is so," Richard replies. "Master Cromwell has given strict instructions that no 'ladies' are to be brought in."

"Bugger!" Suffolk is not happy. "Why, even Cardinal Wolsey used to ship in a few whores. '*My sweet little Magdalenes*' the old rogue used to say. I remember one night ... we had this girl in who could turn cartwheels ... stark naked, and the cardinal leapt to his feet, and did a wild Norfolk jig with her!"

"It is a pity he is gone," Cromwell says, as he joins them. "I seem to recall you keeping very quiet when the king showed him disfavour."

"At least, I did not speak against him, Master Thomas," Suffolk says. "Unlike some, who I wager are not invited here tonight. Old Boleyn and his son, were poisonous, and Harry Percy asked to deliver the arrest warrant, personally. Even the Duke of Norfolk was a greater sinner against Wolsey than I. You know that opposing the king gets you nowhere."

"True." Cromwell keeps his thoughts to himself. Since that black time, he has seen to it that Harry Percy, Duke of Northumberland, has had nothing but bad luck. He is deeply in debt, and has seen his lands shrink, by half their worth. Now, thanks to Cromwell, Thomas Boleyn, Henry's leading courtier has taken a great fall. He may be the king's father-in-law, but his power over Henry Tudor shall be diminished from now onwards. "I stood by Cardinal Wolsey, and see how King Henry treats me."

"You are different," Suffolk replies, colouring up. "You had less to lose, and Henry always likes a …"

"Commoner?" Cromwell smiles. "Enough of this talk now. I want to enjoy a fine dinner."

"I have brought Roman wine… fifty years old."

"Ah, something that is even more aged than I," Thomas Cromwell says, wryly. "Look, here is Eustace. Pray, Brandon, do not mock his hat."

"Why should I do … Good God!" Suffolk stifles the urge to laugh, and bows, instead. "As always, Ambassador Chapuys, it is a real pleasure to meet you."

"Ostrich," Chapuys says, "before you feel

the need to ask, Lord Suffolk. They are all the rage in... Turkey."

"Please, call me Charles," Suffolk replies, genially. The little Savoyard is a pleasant fellow, and he does not mind him being a foreigner at all. After all, he thinks, five hundred years ago, his own people were Norman French. "We are all friends here, are we not?"

"Just so... Charles. A fine name, My beloved emperor also bears that name. It is derived from Charlemagne, I believe."

"Really?" Suffolk says. "Do tell me about these ostrich birds, my dear Eustace."

Tom Wyatt finally makes his entrance, and declaims an impromptu verse, concerning the poor, maligned ostrich.

> *"The ostrich is a wonderful bird,*
> *for it lays an egg, shaped just like a turd,*
> *and sticks its head ... o, what a farce,*
> *up its own be-feathered arse."*

"Thomas Wyatt, by God's Holy teeth, but you are just the man for tonight," Suffolk cries. "What was that again? Farce and arse ... you rascal!"

"Sir, you are mistaken," Eustace Chapuys complains. "It only sticks it in the sand!"

*

Two servants clear away the soup bowls, whilst two more carry in huge platters, each bearing a whole sucking pig. Richard claps his hands in appreciation, and belches. He nods an apology to Digby Weller, into whose face he has delivered it, and the young man smirks back at him, and farts.

"Ah, sucking pig!" Eustace Chapuys, who has already downed several glasses of good Italian wine stands, unsteadily. "In the north of Andalusia, they carve this delight up with a pewter plate's edge, to show how tender is the meat."

"Bollocks!" Charles Brandon says. "Five silver shillings says it cannot be done."

"Lend me the coin, and I will bet with you, Brandon," Tom Wyatt says, cheekily.

"A challenge?" Chapuys looks to Cromwell for permission, and he nods his head. "Bring me a plate, and I will serve out the portions in the Spanish way."

A pewter plate is brought, and Chapuys proceeds to dismember each pig, with unbelievable dexterity. As the edge of the plate does its work, each guest receives an expertly butchered helping. Suffolk is delighted at losing his bet, and slaps down the money, at once.

"That was wonderfully done, my dear Chapuys," Will Draper says. "How many times have you done that before?"

"Never, my dear friend," Eustace says, with a little wink. "Though I once saw a servant do it, some years ago."

"Then the bet was a fair one," Suffolk declares. "For Master Eustace has great pluck to try such a thing, unpractised."

"Please, keep your silver, Charles," Chapuys tells Suffolk. "I feel as though I tricked you."

"What, like that alchemist fellow?" Will Draper asks.

"The Grand Master," Chapuys replies, nodding. "He was a very clever man. Had I not guessed his little trick, I would have sung his praises."

"Trick?" Richard tears into his sucking pig. "You mean the fellow was a fraud?"

"It was but one of my little ruses," Thomas Cromwell tells them. "I thought to see who might be foolish enough to fall for his magical gold making box."

"None here." Rafe is struggling to use the new fork properly.

"Why do you say that, my friend?" Will Draper asks.

"Well, Master Tom has just admitted that it was he who set up the trick," Rafe replies. "My Lord Suffolk, myself and Mush could not fund the charlatan, Wyatt lives on fresh air, Digby earns twelve pounds a year, and Miriam would never let *you* invest in so mad a scheme."

"What about me?" Richard asks.

"You do not have the brains, or the money," Mush says, and the table erupts into laughter. "Shall I have them bring out another pig for you, my friend?"

"Oh, how I laugh," Richard tells the young Jew. "Why, I see you do not eat any at all. Are you seeking to lose weight, or…" The sentence peters out to an embarrassed silence. Mush's religion is a closely kept secret, and Richard realises that he was about to speak of it, openly, in front of two who do not know. The penalty for being found in

England, if Jewish, is still death.

Many Jews pose as Spaniards, to evade the law, but every now and then, the common people take it upon themselves to expose a few, and set upon them. Just a few weeks ago, three Jews have been kicked to death, and their bodies hanged from London Bridge. It is not against the law to kill Jews, and this makes for an awkward situation for those *Chosen People* whom Cromwell favours.

" I do not wish to grow as fat as you," Mush says, and the moment is passed. Richard throws a glance at his friend, that is an apology for his crassness, and Mush nods back. It is alright. It is a matter between friends, and to the young Jew, that is a bond that must never be broken.

"A good roast, Thomas," Suffolk says. "Your table is better than Henry's, though you must never tell poor Hal that."

"Of course not," Cromwell replies. "He has already taken my best young men into his own service, and I would rather keep my cook, if I can."

"We may work for the king…" Rafe starts to say, but Cromwell shushes him into silence.

"It is a privilege for me to let him have you, Rafe, and as for Colonel Draper … well, he is his own man. He has ever been thus."

"I am the King's Examiner now," Will Draper tells the jovial gathering, "and must root out corruption and deceit, wherever it impinges on His Majesty's business. That is why it is my unpleasant duty to be here tonight."

"Unpleasant you say?" Eustace Chapuys wonders if he has misunderstood, for English is not his first language, and in his early days, as ambassador, he pretended no knowledge of the tongue at all. "How can you speak of duty, on such a pleasant evening, my dear fellow?"

"I must go where my duty, and my office takes me," Will continues. "I have suspected a plot against the king for some time now, and I am here to bring matters to a head. Will you all swear, here and now, to help me uncover a wicked act, that was aimed at King Henry, but has hurt many others?"

"Of course we will," Rafe says. "For all here, save our friend, Eustace, are sworn to His Majesty. Tell us what is going on, Will, and we are your men."

"Well said, Rafe," Will replies, "but I have heard the same sentiments uttered from the mouths of men who later turned out to be traitors."

"You seem to have our complete attention," Thomas Cromwell says. "Pray tell us what you must, and be damned to the consequences."

*

The rowing boat bobs up and down on the turning tide, and three men lurk under the northern arch of the bridge. They have made up a half dozen torches; stout sticks, wrapped in rags, and dipped in tar. They place them in the prow of the small boat, where they should remain dry.

"Where is the blasted lamp oil, Deakes?" one of them demands. "I told you to bring as much as you could find."

"You are sitting on it, you stupid pintle,"

Deakes growls back. "What else did you think was in the barrel ... brandy?"

"It would burn as well," the third man sneers.

"Only if you two did not drink it first, Hardy," Deakes says.

"Then let us get it aboard, for the tide is on the turn, and it will get ever harder to row against it. We must be there before midnight, do the job, and let the incoming rush sweep us back to Chelsea."

"What if there are guards?"

"It is a private house," Deakes explains, for the tenth time that day. "By ten, everyone will be long abed. We land, take out our tinder boxes, light our faggots, and hurl them into the place. I shall breach the barrel, and toss it in afterwards. The oil will spread across the floor, and help the flames reach every corner. The whole place will go up in minutes."

"What if some escape?"

"Then they escape."

"What if they manage to put out the fire?"

"That is not going to happen, Black Ned. It will burn too well."

"Say one escapes, and sees us?" Black Ned is the more timid of the three, and has a healthy respect for his own neck.

"Not our worry," Deakes says. "Haskins pays only for the house to be torched. If any live, then it is by God's grace, or bloody good luck. They do not know us, nor do they know who it is that we work for. Remember, if caught, keep silent. Haskins will have us taken up by the Hever

Sheriff, and he will let us loose."

"Then it is Lord Boleyn's hand behind us?" Hardy asks. "It is he, or his son, who want us to torch this place?"

Deakes, who has been a professional criminal for all his life, shakes his head in disbelief. He cannot understand how he has fallen in with two such idiots. He shall explain, once more, in language that even a simpleton might understand.

"Forget Tom Boleyn. Forget his idiot son, and forget Haskins," he snarls at them both. "Do this right, and we are all rich men. Get it wrong, and I will slit your bastard throats!"

11 Conflagration

"I must start with the events of several months back," Will Draper tells his small audience. "You will understand why, as my story progresses to its unhappy end. You will all remember the day our Sovereign Lord, Henry, married his queen, and the unhappy remarks shouted from the crowd?"

"We do," Tom Wyatt says, with a little chuckle, "and they were wrong. Anne is *not* French."

"Have a care, sir," Will tells the young poet. "The marriage does not make your position any safer. If anything, it puts you at greater risk. Henry is a jealous fellow, and can easily be brought to hate any who knew Anne Boleyn in her younger days. The king was furious at the shouts, and ordered me to investigate the matter at once. Had he been presented with the culprit there and then, Henry would have strangled him to death, with his bare hands."

"He is powerful enough," Eustace Chapuys mutters, having once experienced a friendly Tudor hug. "Did you find the scurrilous fellow, Will?"

"No, I did not. I had several lines of enquiry to follow. For instance, the fool might have just felt like calling out insults, or he could have been goaded by drunken friends. Then again, and much more likely, he might have been paid to do it."

"Scandalous!" Suffolk says. "Why did you not run the rogue down?"

"I was sent away, to the north of England instead," Will explains. "It seems that there were certain rumours of a rebellion simmering. I spent almost three months chasing after an Irish priest, who had been well paid to cause trouble."

"By whom?" Thomas Cromwell asks. He is as surprised as the rest are, about this sudden revelation. "I heard nothing of such an infamous plot."

"You were not meant to, sir," Will Draper tells him. "The priest was wont to tour Ireland, threatening fire and brimstone, on all who turned away from Rome. He was recruited by a man called Haskins, who paid him to come across the sea, and cause as much trouble as he could, in Yorkshire, Cumberland, and Lancashire. I found incriminating documents on the priest's body, after I had dealt with him."

"Haskins?" Suffolk muses. "I seem to know that name."

"He is one of the stewards on the Hever estate, in Kent," Rafe Sadler says, angrily. "His name often comes across our desks at Austin Friars. He is in the employ of the Boleyns."

"Then one of them acted against the king," Richard Cromwell says. "This is a clear case of treason!"

"That will be hard to prove," Digby Waller puts in. "They will deny it all, and this Haskins fellow will have some explanation, to help him worm his way out of things. A forged paper, or a fancied impersonation, will muddy things up, and the Boleyn family will escape again."

"As you well know," says Will Draper. "For you were in their employ, were you not, Master Weller?"

"I was," Weller admits, with a cheeky grin. "I knew their schemes, well enough, and took their silver."

"At my instigation," Thomas Cromwell says.

"Yours?" Chapuys is beginning to lose his way. "You set one of your own men to work for these people, *against* you?"

"Master Cromwell knew that Tom Boleyn, and his son, were plotting against us," Digby Weller explains. "I went to them, in secret, and pretended to be a turncoat. I took their silver, and fed them a few silly bits and pieces, to make me look trustworthy to them. Later, when Master Cromwell set up his own trick, I was able to convince them of the authenticity of Aldo Mercurius, and his gold making box. I warned them that Master Cromwell meant to discredit the alchemist, then buy the wonderful secret for himself."

"You cunning old dog!" Eustace Chapuys cannot hide his admiration for his old friend's clever ways. "You show the prize, then seem to toss it aside. Poor Boleyn must have thought himself so clever at outwitting you."

"Just so." Will Draper sees that they have, with the exception of Richard Cromwell, all perceived the trick. "Boleyn went to his trusted spy, Digby Weller, and told him to arrange a meeting with the alchemist. Master Digby consented, and the interested parties met. Mercurius played his part well, and even tried to squeeze more money out of the father."

"That was what clinched it," Digby tells them, grinning widely. "The greed of the alchemist fed his own, and Boleyn agreed to pay over seventy thousand pounds. Then he added a proviso, which made things more awkward. He gave a promissory note to Aldo Mercurius, witnessed, and sealed. The money would be handed over, only on completion of the task."

"Which meant a three month wait, to make it plausible," Will Draper puts in.

"That is so. We hid our fraudulent alchemist away, and I acted as go-between, giving updates on the manufacture of the gold making box. Right from the start, there was a problem. George Boleyn was sure Colonel Draper would sniff out the plan, and alert Henry. You see, old Boleyn meant to turn out gold at a steady rate, and become the richest man in England, without anyone realising, until it was too late."

"So they decided to send me up north?" Will says. He is unsure on this point, and is glad to let Weller clear it up.

"Not at first. George suggested that he hire some thugs to murder you down some dark alleyway, but I said this would cause further investigations, and that George would be a certain suspect. Then I suggested that *Monsignour* had you sent away. I am sorry, but it was that ... or your murder, Colonel Draper."

"I see." Will nods his understanding. Had he remained behind, he would have discovered that it was Digby who was spreading rumours about Queen Anne, and writing pithy slogans on the palace walls. That might have led him to the alchemist plot, and caused his own assassination. "Then I seem to have had a lucky escape."

"I meant to warn you, Will," Tom Wyatt pipes up. "George tells any who will listen, that he will get even with you, one day. I played with him as a child, and he was a very strange little boy. He hated anyone who smiled at his sisters, Anne, and Mary, and took revenge on any who upset his petty minded plans."

"All children can be like that," Eustace Chapuys reminds the company.

"Remember Chuppy?" Wyatt tells them. They all recall the funny little dog, owned collectively by Anne's ladies-in-waiting, so named because it reminded them of Chapuys. Only the ambassador does not know the tale of what happened to his namesake. "How it fell from a high window? George was alone with Anne, and she refused him some trifle. He kicked the poor beast through the window, to its death."

"Good God!" Rafe Sadler gasps. He is a great lover of dogs, and cannot believe such cowardliness. "What could provoke any man to so vile an act? How did the queen upset him to such an extent?"

"That is not for me to speak of," Tom Wyatt replies, his voice flat, and emotionless. "Suffice it to say, he *will* do something, my friend. Trust me."

"Chuppy?" Eustace Chapuys mutters to himself. English humour will always evade him.

"I will watch out for myself," Will says. "Besides, I have a recruit to the office of King's Examiner, who can mind my back."

"Some northern ruffian?" Rafe asks.

"Of sorts," Will replies. The boy, a merchant's son from Skipton, will train up in the art of investigation, rather than soldiery, but he will become a fine officer, and take some of the load from Draper's shoulders. He is lodged in a room at Draper's House, down by the river, and is already a firm friend of Miriam's, and little Gwyllam. "I mean him to learn the art of detecting felons, by their acts, and by their smell. I can always smell a bad apple, my friends."

"Continue your tale, Will," Thomas Cromwell urges. He is still in urgent need of seventy thousand pounds, and wants all the facts from the King's Examiner. "We are all fascinated as to how it concludes."

"I have a clue," Tom Wyatt says. He sniggers, and tells them how old Boleyn has come back to court, a much changed fellow. They listen, politely, for a moment, but Cromwell shows no surprise at Boleyn's new leaf, and the poet's revelations fall flat.

"How does the rest of your story go down?" Rafe asks.

"Simple enough to tell," Will continues. "The Grand Master, after being in hiding for three months, resurfaces, and sends word that the great box is finished, and awaits only payment. He claims that the crafts people, and the workmen want their pay. Seventy thousand pounds must be produced. A king's ransom, for an imaginary wooden box."

"Thomas Boleyn has been diverting treasury funds for months," Thomas Cromwell tells all those present. "He stole the seventy thousand, and sent it off."

"Outside Folkestone, a troop of heavily

armed men appeared, and stole the cart loaded with money."

"Yes, I was going to hand the bounty over to the alchemist, Aldo Mercurius, who was to pass it on to Master Cromwell," Digby Weller confirms. "It was to be such a straightforward transaction. Then these fellows came out of nowhere."

"As if they knew of your coming?" Will asks. Digby shrugs his shoulders, and addresses the entire room.

"The plan went perfectly, until then. I had only six men with me, and we faced levelled muskets, and pistols. Had I fought, we would all have died, and the gold would have gone anyway."

"I am not blaming you, Digby," Cromwell says.

"Oh, but I am," Will Draper snaps. "Who knew about the payment? Thomas Boleyn, George, and you?"

"The alchemist knew, as did his assistant, and Master Cromwell, of course" Weller replies.

"They would not steal what was being freely given," Will suggests. "Anyone else?"

"There is Haskins, I suppose," Digby Weller replies. "He might have told any number of folk."

"Besides," Eustace Chapuys puts in, "was not the plan still a good one? Boleyn loses his money. Money he has taken from King Henry, and money which the king will want to have back?"

"Yes. I have old Tom Boleyn under control now," Thomas Cromwell says. "He knows that I know of the theft, and I have loaned him the seventy thousand, to keep him from the block. In this way, he ceases to be a political threat. There is but one fault with my plan. I do not have the money."

"Ah, I see it now," Eustace Chapuys announces. "You call us here, so that we might resolve your financial problem. I will give you all the ready money I possess, my dear friend, as will these others, I am sure!"

"Would that we few had that much," Will says. "Miriam can find ten thousand, and Mush says he has another three. I doubt that, between us, we can raise above fifteen or sixteen thousand pounds."

"Then I am finished," Cromwell says.

*

"It is darker than I thought it would be," Hardy, a tough, pox marked Kentish man mutters.

"It is night, you fool, What else would you expect?" Deakes growls across the width of the boat. He is the cleverest of the three, and their natural leader on such raids. "Now, keep rowing. Pull hard on the left oar. We need to be getting towards the bank."

"Is there a jetty?" Black Ned's hands are sweating, and slipping on the shaft of his oar.

"God's teeth, Ned, are you mad?" says Deakes. "We run up on the river bank, further up, and come upon the house from the blind side. There, see the place?" They stare at the dark outline, and put in a couple more fast strokes of the oars. The boat's prow runs onto the muddy shore, and they drag it further up, to save it from being whipped away by the strong tidal pull. Later, that same pull will carry them back, under the looming shape of London Bridge, and to the safety of the Chelsea shore. From there, they need only stroll past Utopia, and disappear into the stew of taverns and whore houses that adjoins Westminster.

"Tinder, lads," Deakes commands, and his comrades crouch down, out of any breeze, and start their tinder boxes smouldering. A spark shows that one has been successful, and he blows the spark into a small gutter of flames, and then holds it to one of the well tarred torches. The oil and tar soaked rags catch, at once, and the first torch gutters into life.

*

John Beckshaw cannot sleep. He has never been more than ten miles from Skipton in all his life, and finds the move to London to be most unsettling. With his father's consent, he is to become an officer with the King's Examiner's Office, and learn his craft under the tutelage of Colonel Will Draper. He is King Henry's own Special Examiner, and Beckshaw feels privileged to be at his command.

The Drapers have been very kind to him, and provided him with his own, small room on a lower floor, and the help of a servant, as needed. The food is magnificent, and the company delightful, but he is still unsettled. He is worn out, and yet, he wonders why he cannot close his eyes.

Finally, he decides to get up, and take a breath of night air, to see if it will help him go off to sleep. He goes downstairs, and eases open a ground floor window. He looks out, and imagines that he sees a boat gliding past the foot of the garden. He rubs his eyes, then looks again. It is not a dream, or a trick of the moonlight. A rowing boat, with three men aboard has grounded, just a little way down the shore line.

He knows this should not be, and crosses to the big chest of drawers by the front door. It is the first thing Colonel Draper has shown him; the whereabouts of the house's various fire arms, in case of trouble. He pulls open the top drawer, and takes out two loaded, and primed, pistols. Then he opens the front door, and strides outside. It takes a moment for his eyes to adjust, and he is almost acclimatised to the darkness, when a torch flares into sudden life on the riverbank. Then another, and another.

Even now, John Beckshaw does not quite understand the very real danger, so does not turn to shout for help. Instead, without reasoning things through, he marches towards the source of the blazing torches. It is only when he is within a few yards that he realises their intent, and he curses them for scoundrels.

The three men rush up to the house, where it stands in almost absolute darkness, and are amazed to find a window, open to the elements. Deakes does not hesitate, but hurls his blazing torch into the building. Black Ned follows suit, and Hardy adds to the conflagration. Then, the small barrel of lamp oil follows.

"Hey, you men!" a voice cries from the darkness. "Stand fast!"

The oil splashes, and spreads across the ground, bursting into flames as it goes. In moments, the lower floor is a roaring inferno, and the three men roar their approval to one another, and turn to flee the scene. It only then that they realise there is someone almost upon them. There is a single pistol shot, from close by, and Hardy pitches backwards, with a ragged, bloody, hole punched in his forehead.

Deakes ducks low, and races for the boat, whilst Black Ned makes, what will prove to be, a fatal mistake. He pulls his knife, and runs at the young man who has appeared from nowhere, and shot dead his comrade. John Beckshaw has killed his first man, and his blood is racing. He sees a second dark shape coming at him, and sees the glint of steel by the firelight. He raises the second pistol, tries to keep his eyes open, and squeezes the trigger.

Black Ned screams in pain, as the lead ball smashes into his left shoulder, and sends him spinning around. He falls to one knee, and does not realise that the nearby timber and brick frame is twisting, and falling, because of the intense heat. A large section of masonry tumbles down, and crushes him into the ground.

John Beckshaw staggers back from the flames, cursing, as the entire structure is engulfed. He retreats to the river edge, and looks for the third man. Both pistols are now empty, so he reverses them, ready to use them as clubs. The boat is already well away from the river bank, and the surviving arsonist is heaving himself aboard. Beckshaw curses again, but this time, in pure frustration. His quarry has eluded him.

*

"Bastard!" Deakes snarls, as he gains the safety of the rowing boat. "Who goes for a walk with a brace of pistols?" Still, he is free, and the house is already collapsing in a great, smoking heap of twisted timbers, and red bricks. "More money for me, lads. I told you to watch yourselves!" He laughs, insanely, and waves at the young man who is shaking a fist at him, and cursing him to Hell.

"Go and be damned!" Deakes yells back, and laughs at his assailant's fury.

The little boat hit's the turbulent mid-river, and starts to turn in a tight circle. Deakes grabs at an oar, and searches for the second, in the darkness. It is slipping from the rowlock, and he makes a lunge. It slips from his cold finger tips, and is swirled off in the strong tidal current.

"Bastard!" he says for the second time that night. He leans into the single oar, two handed, to keep him away from the northern bank, and lets the river take him back where it will. The current is in his favour, and the little craft bobs away from the scene of his crime, and carries him back to the looming shape of London Bridge. John Beckshaw, Deakes' young Nemesis in the night is left far behind.

The boat sweeps on, until it comes to the arch of the bridge, where the water is most turbulent. Deakes uses the oar to fend the boat off from the stone pillars, and fails to see a snag of fallen tree trunk, and accumulated debris just ahead. The prow strikes it, and the boat judders and swings about, pitching Deakes into the choppy water. He clings onto the oar, and scrabbles at the stone foundations of the bridge. If he can get a good grip on the rough stones, he should be able to climb up the arch, and work himself onto solid ground.

He is just coming to this happy conclusion, when the boat swings back with the tide, and smashes into the bridge twice, in rapid succession. Deakes is caught between solid stone, and wooden prow. The first blow crushes his chest, and the second knocks his brains out. His lifeless corpse gets snagged on the bridge's roughly hewn masonry, whilst the small craft breaks loose, and swirls off into the night.

*

Back on the river bank, people in the surrounding houses are waking up, and rushing out to see what can be done. They stand, and watch, as the entire building is consumed. One kind soul sees John Beckshaw standing aside, as if in a shocked state, and fetches him a blanket. As he is wrapped in it, he begins to cry.

"Sweet Jesus, what will the master say?" he cries. "He left me in charge, and I have let him down. God curse the day I ever came to this wicked town!"

"Hey, Jenkins!" the merchant who lives several doors down calls. "This fellow has a pistol shot in the head!"

The kindly Master Jenkins eases the spent pistols from John's grasp, and leads him off. He must find someone in authority, and let them know what has come about.

"I shot him down," John Beckshaw admits, with his hands shaking. "There is another one, dead, under the rubble. I shot him too. The third escaped. Had I another pistol, I might have shot him also."

"Dear God, man, hush," Master Jenkins, who is a friend to the Drapers says. "Keep silent, until Thomas Cromwell is informed of the way of things. We do not want you hanged over this, boy!"

"Hanged?" Beckshaw is confused. "But one was burning down the house, and another came at me with a knife."

"That's it, lad. Self defence," Jenkins advises. "That is the way to go for now. Master Kelly, can you set up a chain of buckets, to get the flames under control? We do not want them to spread, and burn down the whole of London, do we?"

"God forbid," Kelly says, as he crosses himself, and starts organising the crowd.

*

"What is it, Crompton?" Henry has been playing cards into the late hours, and wonders why courtiers are running about all over the palace. "Why are they packing my treasures?"

"Fire, Your Majesty," the courtier reports. "The City Guard report a huge conflagration, down river. We do not have any details yet, but it is better to be safe now, rather than sorry, later. All your best possessions will be loaded onto barges, and rowed into mid river, if the flames become too menacing."

"Oh, I see. We have a plan then?" Henry throws aside his cards, and calls for his outside clothes to be brought to his bed chamber. "I would ride out, and see this fire, Crompton."

"I doubt that is a possibility, sire," the grovelling courtier tells the king. "Though we could take the royal barge down river, and have a better view?"

"See to it. I enjoy a good blaze. Whose property is it... do we know?"

"No, sire. It is a stretch of river where no nobility live. I believe it is owned by a few rich merchants, who seek to build their tawdry houses by the river."

"Then no-one of any importance lives there?"

"Apart from Colonel Draper, of course," George Boleyn's wife says from the bed, where she is slipping on a stocking. It is her second visit to the king, and once again, her dubious honour is spared at the crucial moment. "George is always going on about 'those rats who inhabit the river bank'. His wife bought a great big house there, last year, I think."

"Have George found, and taken to Westminster Palace," Henry says, as casually as he can to Sir Edward Crompton. "He has been dunning poor Colonel Draper for some weeks, and I hope he has not arranged for something foolish to be done."

"George cannot arrange a swive in a whore house, Hal," the woman says. "Come back to bed, for you won the last hand of cards, and I must pay the price... in the French way." Henry considers the delightful offer, but he has had his fill of the elusive lady, who never quite delivers what is promised, and would much prefer to see a good fire.

"Have the barge ready at once," he declares. "Let us see if we can be of some assistance."

"From afar, sire," Crompton begs. "You must not endanger yourself, for the queen's sake. She is close to her time, and must not be given any sudden shocks. She must remain calm."

"Then tell her to stop moaning about this lady and I," the king says. "A man cannot go without creature comforts for more than a week or two. Does she want me to suffer some internal hurt?"

"Queen Anne is unreasonable, sire," Crompton agrees, "but it is the way with these things. Ladies who are in this condition, cannot control their feelings."

"Nor can I, My Lord," George's wife simpers from the huge bed. "Will you leave me unsatisfied, yet again?"

"Shut up, and get dressed, at once, Lady Jane," the king tells her. "We are going to watch a fire!"

*

The dining room of Austin Friars is stunned

into silence, at Thomas Cromwell's admission. He cannot find seventy thousand pounds, and it will ruin him with the king. Chapuys is horrified, because he has come to think of his friend as being almost invincible, and cannot see what England will do without such a man at the helm. Will drains his wine glass, and bangs it down o the table. Everyone jumps, and turns to look at him his face is set into a contemptuous smile.

"Very well. I see you will not speak up," he says, "so I will do it for you, gentlemen. My story is almost finished. I rather hoped that it would not be necessary to tell all, but I see that there is a certain lack of moral courage abroad. Last chance."

All eyes remain riveted on Will Draper.

"Then you leave me no choice," he says. "I must accuse, where I may."

12   The Gordian Knot

"Once, when I was faced with a difficult problem, Master Cromwell showed me one of his books. It was in Latin ... a language I am familiar with ... and it was about a man who lived, even before the great Roman emperors. His name was Alexander of Macedon, and he conquered the whole world, from Greece to Italy, and from Africa to India. He even trounced the mighty Persians."

"You remember your history," Tom Wyatt says. "I prefer Greek love poems."

"From which you steal all your best lines," Rafe Sadler says, rather sharply. "Go on, Will, I for one, wish to hear this tale out."

"He was presented with the Gordian Knot, which tied a cart to a post, and was said to be an unfathomable puzzle. The one who could unravel the knot, would rule all Asia, it was said." Will pauses, for Richard Cromwell to keep up. "Some claim he cut the knot, but that was no real answer, was it, my friends? The intricate knot would not then have been unravelled. One who lived at the time claims that Alexander the Great solved the problem, and unfastened it, quite easily. He did this by removing the pin which secures the yoke to the pole of the chariot, then pulling out the yoke itself. The knot, thus removed of its central core, simply falls apart."

"Then you know how to unravel your own particular Gordian Knot, Will?" Mush asks. He has listened to all that has been said, and perceives that there is one amongst them, who is not a true friend after all. One amongst them who is nothing more than a traitor.

"As do you, Mush," Will replies. "Think on what I set you to do, those months ago. I was being banished from London, and told you of my fears. Of how I thought my place was being taken in Master Cromwell's affections."

"Of course. You asked me to keep an eye on Digby. You thought him to be up to no good."

"And did you do as I asked?" Will Draper asks his friend.

"I did, and soon found out that it was he who wrote the slogans, at the master's instigation. Then I found out that he was meeting up with George Boleyn, and even the father, several times a week. I went straight to Cromwell, who assured me that he knew all about it. Digby Weller was working for old Boleyn, but at our request, and was instructed to get into their favour."

"Which you did, Digby." Will says to the young man.

"Very well indeed, if I may say so myself," Digby Weller responds. "They suspected nothing. I was able to get them to trust me, and so fall for Master Cromwell's plot."

"Yes, my friend. You were excellent at playing a double game. That is why you are the solution to my Gordian Knot!"

"I am?" Digby smiles and shrugs his shoulders. "I regret that I do not have your learning, Colonel Draper, so do not understand all this nonsense about Greek kings, and knots. If you mean I was the link that tied Boleyn to Master Cromwell, then yes, I freely admit it to you."

"Excellent, Will Draper replies. "Then let me

remove the pin from the yoke, and see how this knot unravels."

*

"Row me ashore!" Henry demands. Sir Edward Crompton fusses about, begging the king to take care, but Henry is on an adventure, and intends seeing it out. Less than thirty feet away, there is a smouldering ruin, and a crowd milling about, damping down the last of the flames. "Can you not see that there are bodies, sir? Look there, under sheets. Then that lad, who the City Watch seem to have hold of, and there … that person is known to me. Ashore, now, you dogs, or I will have you all flogged."

"Does he never give it a bloody rest?" one of the royal oarsmen mutters. "He treats us like galley slaves."

"Yes," his companion replies, softly, "though the money is pretty good, and we get to go to all the big events."

The barge grounds, and Henry jumps out, into a foot of muddy water. He is fond of doing this, as he believes it makes him look heroic, rather than like a big man with muddy shoes.

Henry splashes ashore, with Crompton, and a half dozen armed guards, following. They too must ruin their boots in the thick Thames mud, and yet get no allowance for it.

"Good citizens!" Henry's voice blasts out, and everyone turns to stare. "Your king is amongst you. Have no fear. Now, what is going on here."

"Going on?" a beautiful young woman

emerges from the crowd, and waves her fists in fury. "Are you some kind of buffoon? I will tell you what is going on …er… if it please Your Majesty, I mean."

"We have met," Henry says, staring down into Miriam's blushing face. He never forgets a pretty girl, and this one, olive skinned and fine, is prettier than most he has seen.

"Mistress Miriam Draper, sire," she says, with a swift curtsey. "My husband is your Royal Examiner. Will Draper, sire."

"Of course. Dear Will." The king wonders at how often the man, or his name, is cropping up, of late. "He is my strong right arm. Now, what is afoot, my poor girl?"

"Arson, sire," Miriam replies, waving her arms at the bodies under the sheets. "These rogues came ashore before midnight, with torches, and lamp oil. Then they set about burning down the house I was having built next door to our own. Our guest, John Beckshaw came upon the felons, even as they set to their task. He shot down one, and the second came at him with a knife. So, John shot him also. Then he chased the third rogue into the river, where he escaped."

"Three against one," Henry mutters. He does love to hear of such heroism. "Why, I once rode into the entire French army, four thousand against twenty four thousand, and scattered them to the winds. Bring the lad here!"

"They have arrested him … for murder, sire," Crompton splutters.

"Then un-arrest him," Henry commands, and the four City Watchmen melt away. "Come here fellow. I see you have won the fray, but did not save Mistress Miriam's house from burning."

"Alas no, sire," John Beckshaw bows, almost down to the ground. "Though I am grateful those wicked fools did not see their mistake. They burned down an empty shell of brick and timber. Had they reached Colonel Draper's home, twenty people, or more, would have perished."

"Crompton, bring a bag of gold for this fellow, at once!" The king is delighted, and demands to hear every detail of the fight, then personally gives the young Yorkshireman a purse, with ten pounds in it. "I am sure Draper will reward you too."

"Sire, he already has. The colonel has inducted me into his office, and I am to be a King's Examiner … after suitable training, of course."

"Damned fine show," Henry says. "Where is your husband hiding, madam?"

"Dining with Master Cromwell, sire, at Austin Friars," Miriam replies. "Has Your Majesty dined?"

"Not since dinner," he says, and I have *exercised* since." It is a slight exaggeration, to make himself look the stud in everyone's eyes.

"Then you must come in, dry your feet, and try some of my pies and tarts," the girl says. "I make the best tarts in London."

"Do you deliver them with a kiss, Mistress Miriam?" the king says, like an adolescent boy.

"Why, sire, I see you have brought along a lady for that part of the business," Miriam replies, saucily. "Lady Jane Boleyn is welcome in my house, though I would not allow her slack jawed husband to cross my threshold, lest I take a stick to his back."

"Oh, yes, I almost forgot," Henry grumbles. "Crompton, pay heed to me. When they have George Boleyn, take him to the Tower of London instead, where we shall speak with him anon. It will throw a fright into the little fool."

"Sire, Lord Wiltshire will be most annoyed," Crompton says, without thinking.

"Lord Wiltshire can kiss my bloody arse," Henry snaps. "Now, ladies… shall we sample these tarts?"

*

"You are the pin, Master Weller," Will says. "You saw how well you were able to tie together both Cromwell, and Boleyn. You used your position to trick the one, and gain prestige with the other."

"Why not?" Digby Weller asks. "A man must make his way in the world."

"Not as fast as you do, sir," Will replies. "You ruin Queen Anne's reputation for fun, then profit by it, when Cromwell comes a-calling. You see that you can get on, and become friends with all at Austin Friars. Then you go to Master Cromwell, and suggest that you try to infiltrate the Boleyn camp. It was that way about, was it not, Master Tom?"

"Well … yes, now I think on it. It was Digby who first suggested it, and volunteered, because he was unknown to them," Cromwell agrees. "I thought it a cunning idea."

"It was. Digby Weller was the lynchpin that held you together. He could see who was going to come out on top, and side with the winner. Had Boleyn outsmarted you, he would have been *his* man."

"I see." Cromwell feels like a fool.

"Once he saw the trick worked, and men would believe his winning talk, and open smile, the next step was easier. How to steal seventy thousand pounds, and get away with it."

"What, Digby has the money?" Richard growls. "Why, he never even stands a round of drinks!"

"No, Richard, he does not have the money," Will says. "How could a fellow of such low birth hope to conceal such vast wealth?"

"He could not," Richard says.

"Correct. He knew when the money was to change hands, and how many men it would take to rob the entourage. Because he was trusted by both sides, Digby Weller even knew that he would remain unsuspected. All he needed, was an accomplice, with enough power to raise a strong, well armed, band of men, and the ability to hide the money away, until the hue and cry dies down." Will Draper sighs, and shakes his head in sorrow. "There was such a man, of course. A man in a high position, trusted by all those around about him; but would he remain loyal to his friends, or would he fall in with the plan, and help steal the money?"

"Name him, Will" Rafe Sadler demands. "Let us know who the rascal is."

"Who here is desperate enough to try and

cheat Thomas Cromwell?" Will replies. "Oh, they might claim that it was only against the Boleyns that they acted, but they have not offered to return the seventy thousand, have they? Even now they know the difficulty that Cromwell finds himself in, he remains silent."

"You have no proof of this," Digby Weller snaps. "The robbers are long gone."

"Yes, but not far," Will says. "For they are local Folkestone men, raised by their master, at short notice… are they not, My Lord Suffolk?" Charles Brandon is white with fright, and does not know what to do. At last, he sees that he is undone. The duke decides to confess to a slight misjudgement, and lay the real blame elsewhere.

"I was taken unawares," Brandon stutters. "Digby Weller came to me, and said there was the chance to ruin Boleyn. I did not think it would hurt you, Master Cromwell. I swear, on my life. I found the men, and set up the robbery, thinking that the Boleyns would be made to look like fraudsters in Henry's eyes."

"I gave you the chance to confess," Will Draper tells him. "I asked if any wished to say anything. You chose to keep silent, hoping I had no proof. Well, I have. You paid off your wine merchant, and your tailor this afternoon. They were owed over eight hundred pounds. You even boasted that there was plenty more where that came from. The harbour master in Folkestone is in my wife's employ, and reports that you have been settling other debts too. I do hope you have not spent too much of Master Cromwell's money, My Lord!"

"About two thousand," Brandon confesses.

"You damned fool, Charles," Tom Wyatt says. "Did you not realise that you would be found out?"

"Weller swore that no one would ever realise," Suffolk confesses. "He talked me into it. I was to hold his share, until he could arrange for it to be taken over to France. Once I took the first, stupid step, I could not turn back from the allotted course. I am truly sorry, Master Cromwell, but I meant you no harm at all … rather, I wished to help you, by ruining the Boleyns."

"I believe you," Thomas Cromwell says, for he knows how Suffolk's mind works, hopping from one thought to another, without any real cohesion. "Where is the money hidden now?"

"Under lock and key at Westhorpe Hall, sir." Suffolk is not a clever man, and wonders how he ever thought to get away with it. "I can only say I was taken in by a sharper witted fellow than I. Your servant, Digby Weller, knows how to weave a web about you, and no mistake. What will happen to me?"

"You should be hanged," Eustace Chapuys says, in a most un-diplomatic way. "Your actions may have ruined Thomas Cromwell, the finest minister since Cardinal Wolsey, and left the royal treasury depleted, at a time of great need. Your childhood friend, the king, would have your head for this day's work, I am sure, My Lord Suffolk."

"Dear God, Cromwell!" Tom Wyatt begs, with a nervous laugh. "Charles is a fool… a damned fool, of course, but he meant *you* no harm. Once he had slept on it, he would have quietly confessed, and returned what is left. Am I not right, Brandon?"

"You are, Wyatt, I swear it, on my life," Suffolk says, grasping at the lifeline thrown by an old friend. "How could I ever betray such a good fellow, and so generous a man as you, Master Thomas?"

"Enough of this, My Lord Suffolk," Tom Cromwell says, gruffly. "Colonel Draper will collect my money tomorrow. I will call the shortfall a loan, between friends, and add it to your account. You will return to the country, and remain there, until my temper has cooled. Do you understand?"

"I do, sir, and beg your humble pardon," Suffolk says. "I shall never let you down again."

"You will never have the chance," Rafe Sadler snaps. "Keep well away from court, sir, for you will find nothing but cold countenances there. In fact, I will speak with the king, and suggest a diplomatic posting for a few months. Somewhere cold, and inhospitable, I think. The Swedes have asked us for another ambassador, since the last perished of the cold."

"As you say, Master Sadler," Brandon replies. He is relieved to get off so lightly, and consoles himself with the thought that his tailor, at least, will extend him more credit for a while. "I shall not demur."

"Now for you, Weller," Thomas Cromwell says. "I have a mind to deal with you most harshly, but cannot act out of mindless anger. You must, at least, have a chance to speak for yourself, for I do doubt most readily that you will find an advocate amongst our fellow diners, who would defend your vile actions."

"Nor would I trust their wit, nor their wisdom," Digby Weller replies, tartly. He stands, and crosses to the fire, where he positions himself, like a witness standing in a court of law. "I start out by reminding you that I did not seek out a position with your household, Master Cromwell. It was you who sought me out. In my comments about the queen, you saw an advantage, and decided to use me against Her Majesty. Everyone in this room knows that Anne and her family wish to remove you from power, and that you must fight against them, for your very life."

"I do not refute what you say," Cromwell confesses. "I hired you to spread rumours, and upset the Boleyn family."

"Just so. I was good… very good … at it, and Queen Anne wanted Henry to set the colonel onto my track," Digby Weller continues. "It was about this time that I thought to infiltrate the Boleyn fold. I saw what Colonel Draper was about, and suggested to George Boleyn that he might be best put out of the way. He would have had you killed, sir, but I advised against the action, most strongly. Instead, I suggested a trip to the north of the country, for a few months."

"Thank you for that," Draper says, coldly. "You seek to make it sound that you saved me. I would have dealt with George Boleyn easily enough, and still found out about you, fellow."

"Then let us say that it suited my purposes," Weller replies with a casual shrug. "I fed useless information to Boleyn, and they thought I was their man inside Cromwell's circle. I took a wage from my master, and brought any bribes back to Austin Friars. You see, Mush had told me the rules. A portion for the house, and a portion for Master Cromwell. I made over a hundred pounds for my fellow Austin Friars agents, and received less back."

"You received our support, and free board and lodging, as well as your twelve pounds a year," Cromwell says. "In time, you would have prospered, as have all my other young men."

"In time." Digby Weller turns, and spits into the fire, which flares for a moment. "I was born into nothing, and brought up into nothing. Yet I am cleverer than any noble in court, and able to turn things to my own advantage, by thinking on my feet. I saw, almost at once, that Boleyn was a vain fool, yet still smarter than his idiot of a son. Only Anne has any real intelligence, and that is marred by her haughtiness."

"Is this your defence?" Cromwell asks. "That you did it because those about you were too stupid, or arrogant to stop you?"

"No, sir, it is not." Digby Weller smiles, winningly at his audience. "My defence is a simple one. Not that I did it because I could, but rather that I *had to*. I was compelled by my early life of poverty to make the most of my chances. I was a poor fellow, and simply could not help myself."

"Greed then?" Rafe asks.

"No, it was fear," Digby Weller replies. "I could not face a life of poverty. When Master Cromwell explained his cunning plan to me, I saw all sorts of possibilities. At first, I wondered how to divert a portion of the money into my own pocket. It would not hurt Cromwell, for it was going to be Boleyn money. Then old Tom Boleyn confessed to me that he did not have any ready cash to hand."

"That is true," Thomas Cromwell confirms. "Henry has given them over half of Wiltshire, and a dozen noble titles, and estates. All of which produce a steady income of several thousands of pounds a year. He could not raise seventy thousand in one go. I sought to drive him into borrowing the money, then buying up his markers for a part of their worth."

"Which is exactly what I suggested to him," Digby Weller confirms. "I thought to earn a few commissions, if I introduced him to a Flemish banker or two, but he refused my offer. He told me that he had a better, cheaper, way of raising the money, and that I was to keep an eye on the alchemist."

"Who was hidden away in Folkestone, was he not?" Will Draper asks.

"The whole time. I saw to it that he, and his friend, were kept comfortable, and reported back, once a week, on how well the work was progressing. You see, we had Boleyn's paper, but could only use it to pay craftsmen, and suppliers. So it was no real use to us. We had to get Boleyn to produce his seventy thousand."

"I realised where he was taking the money from after the first month," Cromwell says. "But by then, it was too late. I could not stop him without my part in the plot being revealed. Henry would have damned us both. So, I listened to you, did I not, Master Weller?"

"You did. I suggested that we let him pay over the seventy thousand, then let him see how he was duped. Once the money was gone, Boleyn would be trapped. Master Cromwell could pretend to discover the shortfall then, and offer to loan him the money. In this way, Boleyn was in our power, and all we had to do was repay the stolen thousands."

"A sound plan, Digby," Mush says, speaking for the first time. "What went wrong?"

"My personal need for wealth," Digby Weller replies, and shrugs his shoulders. "I suddenly thought … why return the money at all? If it was stolen … *really stolen*… I could take at least a half share for myself. Boleyn would still be ruined, and could say nothing about it, without incriminating himself in the original embezzlement. You see my thinking, Mush? Boleyn is caught, and all Cromwell needs to do is replace the missing seventy thousand pounds. I thought he had it, locked in his strong room. Then, it only remained for me to find another, as dishonest as myself."

"I say!" Suffolk is affronted. He, like most nobles, has the ability to alter the truth to suit his own needs, and is already thinking of himself as the wronged party in all of this. He has been, quite innocently, he thinks, led into stealing a fortune from his king, and trying to ruin Cromwell and Boleyn … as if my mistake. "You make me out to be as guilty as you, fellow."

"How can that be, sir?" Digby Weller replies, tartly. "For you are of *noble* blood."

Several of the guests chuckle, and observe the sharpness of the young man's wit. "I merely remark that I needed an accomplice to the crime. A man who could raise a troop of tough fellows, and would then be able to conceal our ill gotten gains."

"Then Lord Suffolk was the ideal person," Eustace Chapuys says, sharply. "For he has plenty of armed men at his disposal, and several fortified castles, and great homes."

"My only worry was whether I could trust him, or not," Digby Weller continues. "Then I reasoned it out. If he cheats me, it is a simple matter to drip poison into the right ears, and he is ruined, and must either flee, or surrender to Henry. As he would rather wish to live a life of ease, he would give me my share, without demur."

"You had all the salient points covered," Will Draper says to him. "Except for one. Such a plan can only work if everyone has faith in you. Boleyn did not suspect. Cromwell was taken with you, and the rest of Austin Friars thought you a most personable sort of a fellow. I wager even the Duke of Suffolk found you a seemingly trustworthy young man. Only I mistrusted you. You were simply too good a sort. To come from so humble a background, and yet be so faithful, and … well, noble sounding did not sit well with my usual suspicious nature. I looked for the flaw, and I found it."

"You knew I was the phantom caller of insults, and message writer," Weller says. "That is all."

"I asked Mush to watch you," Draper says, "but I did not fully trust his opinion either. So, I told Tom Wyatt of my fears, too."

"True enough, Master Cromwell," the poet puts in. "I owe you a great debt, and did not like the idea that this fellow was using you in some way. I started to frequent the same inns as Weller, and have him followed. I soon found that he was working for two masters, as had Mush. Over the months, I came to realise that he was working some sort of intricate game with Aldo Mercurius, but that Austin Friars seemed aware of it, and did not mind. I did not understand what was afoot, but my regard for your clever wit, kept me on my guard."

"Plots, wrapped within plots," Thomas Cromwell mutters. "It is my weakness."

"Then, things began to happen rather quickly." Tom Wyatt takes a deep breath, for he is a friend of Suffolk, and would do him as little harm as possible. "I employ a couple of young fellows, who pass information to me, which I then pass on to Austin Friars. One of these lads spotted Digby Weller calling on the Duke of Suffolk, and passed the news back to me. I kept close to them both, and was actually dining with Charles Brandon when one of his stewards came in, and spoke to him about having enough men ready. My friend, Charles, made out that it was for a hunting trip in Cambridgeshire, but why, I asked him, did he not invite me to chase down his stag? Nobles only, he told me. Though he swore it was so, I feared otherwise."

"As you were right to do," Will Draper says. "For My Lord Suffolk was arranging a heavily armed war party, to steal away the king's gold."

"Boleyn's," Suffolk claims.

"Thomas Cromwell's," Rafe Sadler corrects.

"I took to hanging around Charles' place. Then, by chance, I saw him ride out with his gang of robbers. I followed, and witnessed the whole thing. They surrounded the cart, and drove everyone away at gunpoint. Charles hung back, lest he was recognised, I suppose. Once back in London, I told Will Draper, who bade me hold my tongue, for the time being. I did not know that all was to be revealed here tonight."

"You did well, Master Wyatt," Thomas Cromwell says. "You still have my friendship, for what it is worth. As for you, Colonel Draper, why, I wonder at how devious you have grown these past twelve months. Your cunning mind, and ready wit, knows no bounds, and you have saved the day once more."

"You would have come to the same conclusion," Will replies. "Though I was quicker, because I did not like your Master Digby Weller. His smiling ways did not meet with my tastes, at all."

"Then, there it is," Digby Weller says. "I tricked Boleyn, duped Cromwell, enticed Suffolk, and outthought you all, save a man who comes from the same low background as I."

"No, sir, not the same," Will Draper retorts. "As low, perhaps, but a background that gave me a set of my own morals to follow. There, my report is made, gentlemen. Suffolk will return the money, and you can repay the treasury, Master Thomas."

"Thank you, Will."

"Your servant, sir," Will replies. "Suffolk

must lose his ill gotten gains, and may be banished from court for a while. What of Master Weller? How is the rogue to be punished?"

"Perhaps you can all take a quick vote on my fate, like a jury," Weller sneers. "All you good, and true fellows, who have never done a wrong thing in all of your lives."

"Enough. I rule here in Austin Friars, sir, and it is for me to make the decisions," Cromwell is suddenly cold, and more like the man of old. "The punishment must fit the crime. It can be neither too severe, nor too benign. Are you ready for my judgement, Digby Weller?" Weller shrugs. He has no say in the matter, and must abide by whatever Thomas Cromwell chooses.

"Do what you wish," he says, looking his master in the eye. "For I did no more than you, when you pillaged the French baggage train, or duped a scheming pope, sir."

"You sought to gain fabulous wealth from this," Cromwell tells him. "Therefore, let the opposite come to pass. You came to me with five shillings to your name, no roof over your head, and an empty stomach. You will leave me in the same way."

"Master, I am worth over two hundred pounds, by my own effort," Weller complains. "What of that?"

"Then that is the amount of the fine. You forfeit two hundred pounds, and will not spend another night under my roof. I give you twenty four hours leg bail. If I find you within thirty miles of London, *ever again*, your life is forfeit too."

"Master, may I speak?" Mush steps from his

quiet corner. He has offered little to the proceedings, but now feels compelled to speak out about a man who he calls 'friend'. "Digby Weller has been a good friend to me, these last few months. I grew to trust him, which is not my usual way. Might I ask a single favour … if only because of my past service to you?"

"Go on." Cromwell knows he must accede to Mush, whatever he might ask, or risk losing his devotion. It sorrows him that the young man wishes to plead for Waller, even after the man has betrayed everyone he has come into contact with.

"Let me take Digby Weller across the river tonight," Mush tells them all. "That way, he will not be tempted to stay on the London side. He is a wilful sort, and might be tempted to flout the restrictions my master has placed on him. I will row him over to the south side, and see him well on his way."

"And slip him a bag of gold, no doubt," Rafe Sadler sneers.

"Is that really any of your business?" Mush Draper replies, fiercely. "You go on about protecting Master Cromwell's interests to the point of boring us all to death, but you did not see any of this coming, and I have never yet seen you charge into a life or death fight. It takes more than a lawyer's mind, and a couple of well written writs, to keep Austin Friars together, my friend."

"I hope Master Cromwell can rely on us both, each in our own ways," Rafe replies. "It was never my intention to insult you, Mush. The words came out before my *'lawyer's mind'* had checked them over. It is true what you say. My interest in the whole business ends when the man is out of Master Cromwell's employ, and off Austin Friars' payroll."

"Well said, Rafe," Richard growls. He looks as if he could rip Weller's head from his shoulders, but knows that his uncle is making the right decision. "Digby Weller can spend his penny in any other town, from now on. London is closed to him. Our people will see to that. No inn will shelter him, or bawdy house entertain the fellow. There is not a place where he will find gainful employment, lest it be outside of this city."

"The twenty four hours are already running, Mush," Thomas Cromwell says.

"You may have the loan of one of Miriam's skiffs, my friend," Will tells his brother-in-law. There are three tied up at the jetty. Try not to awaken the household when you take one. Miriam does not like her sleep disturbed."

"Master Cromwell!" The great hall's door is flung back with surprising violence, and one of the more senior servants, is there, sweating and shaking, as if he has run across the city. "A great fire, sir. Down by the riverside. The boy who comes with the news thinks it is close to Colonel Draper's house."

"Dear Christ!" Will leaps to his feet, and runs for the door.

Thomas Cromwell signs for Rafe, and Tom Wyatt to go with him. He will follow, but at a more sedate pace. His running days are long over. Is this the start of it then, he thinks. Have his enemies decided to strike, before he is ready for them?

"I will follow, with as many servants as I can muster, Will," he calls. "God speed you there, and I pray that no harm has come to any of yours!" Will, Tom Wyatt and Rafe Sadler are gone, and Mush looks undecided.

"Carry on, Mush," Cromwell tells him. " Get this perfidious young man out of my city." Mush takes Digby Weller by the elbow, and leads him off. By the time he gets to the waterfront, he will see that the fire is not at Draper's House, but in the unfinished new building, next door.

Thomas Cromwell's servants brings him a warm cloak, and tells him that there are a dozen good men waiting to obey his orders.

"I fear we are too late to help with the fire," Cromwell says to Richard, who has stayed by his uncle's side. "I will go there with James, and a couple of the others. We will take food and drink for those who must be helping."

"And I, uncle?" Richard is not the most quick witted of his followers, but he gets there in the end. "What am I to do?"

"What do you think has happened?"

"An attack on one of our own," Richard guesses. "Houses made of brick do not burn for no reason. They must be torched."

"Then who must we suspect?"

"One of the Boleyns," Richard says.

"Not Tom Boleyn. The old man is in my pocket, for the moment. Nor would Queen Anne attack in this way. She would whisper to Henry, and turn him against us. It is that idiot, George Boleyn."

"What are my orders then?"

"Take these remaining men, and any other of our agents you can raise, and scour London for him." Tom Cromwell thinks for a moment. "It can only be him. Find him, and take him."

"Am I to dispose of the man?"

"No, we dare not kill the queen's brother," Thomas Cromwell replies. "Though I am sorely tempted to it."

"I can have him disappear," Richard explains. "My men can strip his house, and make it look as if he has fled. Then I will cut his throat, and sink his body to the bottom of the Thames."

"I am tempted," Cromwell says, "but, no. Find him, and lock him away in an Austin Friars cellar, or a damp cupboard.

"As you wish, uncle." Richard pauses before leaving. "You know, do you not, that of us all, I am the one who will never question you?"

"I know, Richard," Cromwell replies, smiling at the huge bear of a man. "We are of the same blood." Then a thought comes, unbidden to him. "What if it is not just Will Draper whom they wish to strike against? Where is Gregory?"

"Why, he was staying the night at … the Drapers!"

"Sweet Christ," Cromwell curses, "what has become of the boy?"

13   A King's Fault

The flames are under control, and there is little more than an orange coloured glow coming from the ruin next door. Miriam has ordered fires to be lit in the eating hall, and whatever fresh food there is to be brought out of the pantry. The long table is laid out with several roasted fowl, two game pies, assorted breads and cakes, and a dozen large custard tarts.

The king thinks it is a wonderful, impromptu picnic, and refuses a chair. He will stride up and down the hall, talking to whom he may, and picked up food as he wishes it. Sir Edward Crompton, who has spent several years as a professional fawner to the king, is worried that he might mix too freely with the common herd, and so become less dependant on his coterie of hangers on.

"The fellow does not quite know how to treat Miriam, and her household," Henry confides to the handsome young man at his side. "See how the old fool simpers, and shivers in fear. He thinks I will stop loving him, and find him a more menial task than agreeing with me, all the time."

"Does that not tire you out, sire?"

"Sometimes." Henry scowls at the young fellow, and tries to recall where they have met before. "Have you been named to me, sir?"

"I am Gregory, Your Majesty. He who almost overcame you at the joust, with Will Draper."

"Almost, yes… and there were two of you," Henry remembers his own truth, and slaps Gregory on the shoulder. "You are Thomas

Thomas Cromwell's son. Is he educating you well enough, boy?"

"I live in Cambridge, sire, during school times, where I am being taught Latin, writing, and my mathematics. I shall come home when I am fifteen, and be put to the law, my father says."

"I think not," Henry says. "That would be a waste. I shall speak with your father, and tell him that you must be presented at court, once educated, and that your further education ... at tilting, swordsmanship, and courtly behaviour, shall be entirely at my own expense."

"You are too kind, sire," Gregory says. "Though I would just as soon join the army, and fight your foes in Ireland, and France."

"We are not at war with the French."

"Not yet, sire," Gregory says, with the openness of youth. "My father says that they will not wish to see your greatness grow much more, and will contrive to fight us."

"Does he, by God!" Henry laughs. "Master Cromwell, the statesman, advises me that commerce is better than warfare."

"And so it is, sire," Gregory replies, trying to put his father's words into some sort of order. "I think war is the last resort, in his eyes. Though that does not mean he will not fight. As a young man, he fought the French, in Italy."

"The man has hidden depths," Henry says, and crushes a whole custard tart into his mouth. He starts to choke, and Gregory, untutored in such matters, slaps his back, overly hard. The king coughs out a few morsels, and is able to breath again. "Well done, my dear little fellow. I must appoint you to be my royal back slapper!"

"At your service, sire," Gregory Cromwell says. "Did you see how John Beckshaw killed those scoundrels?"

"Alas, I was here too late. *Lady* Crompton did dither too long at getting my barge ready. I should have rode here."

"I saw, from my bedroom window," Gregory confesses. "I woke up, and looked out, to see three men torching the building site next door. Then John was there, a brace of pistols at the ready. Two shots, and two men down. Then the whole house fell down on the wounded one, and the last man made off in a boat. The last I saw, he was being swept towards the bridge."

"Are you sure, Gregory?" Will Draper is suddenly there, with others from Austin Friars rushing about, looking where they might best give their help. "He went upriver, you say?"

"He did, sir," Gregory affirms. "I saw the boat, taken by the swell, and one man, fighting with the oar."

"Will Draper!" Henry is enjoying every moment. "We have saved your house from these rogues, and driven them away. Pray, as my Examiner, look into things, and see the king's justice is done."

"As you command, sire," Will says, wondering who has been fool enough to let the king become involved in things. "Now, you must be taken to a safe place."

"Not I, sir!" Henry is in full flow. "I am with you. What shall we do?"

"Was anyone else hurt, sire?" Will asks.

"No. I came upon your lovely wife, and her people, and ordered them here, to a place of safety."

"My thanks, sire." Will Draper almost laughs out loud with relief. By the morning, Henry will have driven off the arsonists single handed, and saved Miriam from certain death. "The last felon was being swept away, and did not have control of his boat. I think we might find him past the bridge."

"Exactly my thinking, Colonel Will," Henry says. "Then we must find horses and …"

"There are boats tied up at the jetty, sire," Gregory informs him. "Perhaps we could take one of them, or even board your royal barge?"

"Ah, yes. My barge is here. I forget, in the excitement of the times," Henry says. "Come, we will give chase."

"Sire!" Sir Edward Crompton comes bustling up, arms flailing around, and fingers fluttering. "We must think of Your Majesty's safety. This man might be dangerous."

"Then fetch me a dagger, and be damned to you … you shivering …custard. Come Will, let us get on. Gregory, fetch young Master Beckshaw, for he is also one of my Examiners, I believe."

"Get off, husband," Miriam urges, as she makes an appearance from the kitchens. "It seems I must feed half of the city, at our own cost. See to the king."

"Well said, Mistress Miriam."

"I shall keep your friend safe by my side," she replies, with a cheeky grin. "Until you have need of her again."

"Oh, yes. I forgot. Yes, see to the lady, I pray. It was mere chance that we met, of course. The queen need not know of it, Mistress Miriam."

"Sire, this household is for God, and the king," Miriam says, as she curtseys. "The lady is called Jane. She is a friend of mine, and was merely visiting for the evening."

"Excellent. Will, your wife is … a female Cromwell. She is not his daughter, by any chance, is she?"

"Who can tell, sire," Will replies, ushering them all towards the jetty. "Master Cromwell travelled the world in his youth, and knows how to sew his seeds, like any good farmer." He catches Miriam's eye, and she winks at him.

*

It takes a half hour to get Henry back on the royal barge, and a while longer to urge the twelve rowers into action. It is only when Will draws his sword, and starts tapping a beat with its hilt, that they pick up the stroke, and send the huge barge back towards the mighty span of London Bridge.

"Harder over, you buggers," the shipmaster commands, "else we will ram into the arch. Aha, look there!" He holds up a lantern, and points, eagerly at the huge stone bulwark, that is rearing out of the darkness at them. "See, some poor wretch has done just that!"

Will crosses to the port side, and examines the crushed remains, which have become snagged on the masonry. He leans out of the boat, and is about to cut the shattered corpse free, when Henry comes up alongside him.

"What is it?" the king demands. "Is the rascal taken?"

"By God, sire," Will mutters. "Would you have me drag him on board, or cut him loose?"

"Have one of my fellows tie a rope around the thing, and hoist it on deck," Henry says. "Then, have all three of the bodies taken to Hever, in Kent, and hanged from the ramparts of the castle."

"Hever, sire?" Will Draper sees that the king is of a like mind. "Then you have solved this particular investigation before me?"

"It is only that I am a little quicker witted than you, Colonel Will," Henry replies, seriously. "That is how I was able to best you in the joust the other day. It does not reflect badly on you, being the second cleverest man in England. I knew, at once, that it was down to someone who bore you a great grudge. George Boleyn has been cursing you for months. So, the bodies are a reminder to the Boleyns, that I married the daughter, and not the whole damnable family."

"Well said, sire." Gregory is beside them. "Can I pull the body in, Will? I have never seen an arsonist before… not even a dead one!"

"What of George Boleyn, Your Highness?" Will asks. He already knows the answer, and he must steel himself to it. "Master Cromwell will guess too, and have men out seeking the fellow."

"As have I," Henry replies. "You know I cannot punish George, as I would any other who dares to harm you, and yours. He has the profound good luck to be married to the queen, and she has the even profounder good luck to be married to me. I dare not upset her at this moment. She is about to give birth to my child, and a sudden shock might cause untold harm."

"Then afterwards?" Gregory asks, and they all turn to see what the child means. "Once your child is delivered, might we not punish him?"

"I fear not," Henry says. He is unused to the sort of frank approach that Gregory uses. "By then, he will have covered his tracks, I think. What had you in mind?"

"Haskins," Gregory replies, dropping his voice to a conspiratorial whisper. "He is the Boleyn steward, and George uses him to do his dirty work. My father says he is a dangerous man, and has his name in his bad book. Might we not take him up, and punish him for this?"

"I see," Henry smiles. "If I hang this fellow, it will send a stronger message to Thomas Boleyn."

"A warning," Gregory says, warming to the business of political intrigue. "It will say '*I know you have crossed me, and here is a sign of my great wrath.*' I think they will understand what is meant."

"Excellent. Where is Crompton?"

"We left him behind, sire." Will waves Gregory away, and joins him amidships. "Well, Master Gregory, how does it feel to condemn a man to death?"

"It was a jest," Gregory says, white faced. "I did not think he would agree to …"

"Hang a man without trial?" Will Draper shakes his head in disgust. "You stupid boy. By tomorrow, Henry will have convinced himself that this Haskins fellow was the true guilty one, not the Boleyns, and our task will become harder."

"Our task?"

"To entirely destroy Queen Anne, and all of her kin folk," Will explains, *sotto voce*. "For if we do not, they will do the same to us!"

"Turn about, you bastards!" Henry is slapping the oarsmen about their heads, and urging them to swing the huge royal barge about. "I want Crompton. He has someone to hang for me!"

*

Thomas Cromwell, and Eustace Chapuys arrive, just as most of the neighbours are leaving. They have beaten down the last, glowing embers, and eaten their fill of Miriam's food, in the company of King Henry, his courtiers, and his noble friends. It is, purely by chance, the most egalitarian feast ever seen in Tudor times. The little Savoyard seeks out Miriam, who is holding the baby, Gwyllam, and confirms that she, and the rest, are unhurt.

"It is those who came against us who came off the worst, dear Eustace," she tells him. "They mistook the house, and burned down my new construction. It was only timber and a brick façade which was lost. A few hundred pounds will put things aright again."

"I have enough, if you need a loan," he says, then smiles. He recalls how Cromwell treats her and her family, and knows she is under no hardship.

"Your continued friendship is all we want," she says. "Here, hold my boy for me, whilst I assure Master Tom that we are well."

"What of Will?"

"Already on the river, chasing down the last of them," Miriam replies. "Master Beckshaw was good enough to dispose of the first two. He tells me that he has only ever fired a pistol three times, and has hit his mark on each occasion. Though he does confess it to be more by fool's luck, than intention."

"Miriam, my dear girl," Thomas Cromwell is almost in tears as he sees her. "We will rebuild. Do not worry. I have a good mind to add the cost to Boleyn's debt. In fact, I will. Damn them all to Hell. Boleyn shall repay you, and with interest. That is if Will lets them live after tonight."

"It was an empty shell," she reminds him.

"My dear," Eustace Chapuys interrupts. "They meant to burn you, your child, Will, and all others under this roof to death. Do not take it so lightly."

"My God, yes." Miriam's eyes well with tears at the very idea. "Dear Gwyllam … God rot their souls!"

"Your king has been greatly at fault in this matter," Chapuys tells them.

"Have a care," Cromwell cautions. "Were you English, you would be speaking treason, my friend."

"I speak as I find," Chapuys replies, earnestly. "He enjoys playing his courtiers off, one against the other, and thinks he is being a great diplomat. When all he does is create enmities, where trust should be. He supports Boleyn, and lets him think it acceptable to attack another man's family. In this way, he believes he is strengthening his court, instead of weakening it. Boleyn against Suffolk, Norfolk against Percy, and all of them against Cromwell!"

"It is the way of things," Thomas Cromwell tells him. "The Tudors come from a long line of Welsh lordlings, whose power was derived from raiding, and plotting. It is in their very blood, you see. Henry cannot understand that men can rise above petty politics, and create a strong realm. He thinks that, should we unite, his power will diminish… and he is probably right."

"Then God help you all," Chapuys says, "for Anne Boleyn is about to gain the ultimate power over your Henry. The birth of a son will make her family untouchable, and signal the end of your dream, Thomas. If the worse happens, you must take ship to anywhere within the Holy Roman Empire, where my master will offer you shelter from the tyrannical storm that shall come."

"Emperor Charles will not want a thorn like me in his side," Thomas Cromwell replies. "Besides, I have no intention of losing this particular fight. The king must have a prince, but he does not need a queen. I will fight my corner, when the moment comes."

"And perish?"

"Perhaps. Then you might wish to offer shelter to all those of mine who wish to leave." Cromwell calls to his servants, and gives instructions to them. Miriam's home is a mess, and must be put in good order, whilst her husband is off, about the king's business. By the time he is back, Draper's House must be, once more, in the usual sort of order.

*

"I had nothing to do with that," Digby Weller says, as they step aboard one of Miriam's light boats. It bobs, gently on the Thames, and strains against its mooring.

"I know," Mush Draper replies. "The Boleyns are behind it, I suspect. It is the sort of half arsed tomfoolery that would appeal to George. We will attend to him anon. Sit in the stern, and steer, whilst I row."

"Where do we head?" Weller sits at the tiller, and unties the thick mooring rope from the peg on the jetty.

"Shoreditch, on the farther bank. The tide is still with us, and the rowing should not be too hard." Mush sits, and takes an oar in each hand. Three strokes sends them away from the shore, and into the tidal pull. "What made you do it, Digby?"

"What?" Digby Weller manoeuvres the boat towards the midstream. "Steal the money, or go against Cromwell?"

"Both." Mush wants to understand. "In a year or two, Cromwell would have made you into a gentleman, with a good income, and your own house."

"I did not wish to wait two years," Weller explains.

"He trusted you."

"And I did not play him false … until I had to." Digby sees he must explain more fully. "I will play the part, as long as nothing better comes along. I was willing to trick Boleyn, and give my loyalty to Cromwell, as long as nothing better came knocking on my door. Seventy thousand pounds, Mush. Think of it, my friend. Enough money to last a man two lifetimes."

"Then it was just the money?"

"I suppose so." Weller considers. "I like Cromwell, and dislike George Boleyn, but that does not profit me, other than by a hundred a year. Once I saw how to gain the money, I could not remain loyal to anyone, save myself."

"You have no morality." Mush hears himself saying the words, and almost laughs. For too many morals can get you killed, he thinks. Weller's crime was getting found out. "What of our own friendship?"

"It was real enough," Digby Weller replies. "We are kindred spirits. Whilst I was Cromwell's man, we suited one another, and our friendship grew apace. We had similar thoughts, and similar likes, and dislikes. That is why we became such good friends, is it not?"

"Yes."

"There is still time, Mush."

"For what?"

"Why, for you to row us back to the northern bank," Digby Weller explains. "We can take two horses, and ride for Suffolk's little hideaway. His men know my face, and expect the money to be moved. We can be on a boat to France by first light. Just think what can be done with thirty five thousand pounds each."

"No." Mush does not care to elaborate, or explain how much he owes to Thomas Cromwell. Such a crime would destroy the man, and be the greatest betrayal since Cain felled his brother in the Garden of Eden.

"Sure?"

"Yes."

"Then you have a purse for me?"

"I have a purse."

"Good man. I knew you would stand up to Sadler. He does not understand true friendship." Weller sees they are drifting back to the wrong bank, and leans on the tiller, to force them back towards the Southwark side. "We had some good times, Mush, did we not."

"We did, right enough. " Mush is blowing hard, and seems to be struggling against the tide. "The undertow is strong tonight."

"Really?" Weller sniggers. "Is it not that you are a weakling, old fellow?"

"I am stronger than you," Mush replies. "It is just hard to fight the current."

"You milksop."

"Coxcomb!" Mush snaps back, and they both laugh. "God, but I am going to miss you, Digby. More than I can ever say."

"You can always ride south, one day. I dare say I will be thriving in Sussex, or Surrey. Perhaps I will find a rich widow, or two, to fleece." Digby Weller feels a moment of regret for the tarnished friendship, then shrugs the feeling off. "Watch out, you will have us back where we started."

"Damn it, but I cannot get us into clear

water," Mush confesses. "Let us change over. You show off your professed strength, and I will steer us true."

"Like I said ... milksop," Digby says. "Come, I will lash the tiller. Watch we do not overbalance. You go to the right, and I to the left."

They stand, and cross each other. Mush seems to lose his balance, and snatches at his friend's sleeve, so as not to overbalance the boat. Digby Weller suddenly stares at his friend, and shakes his head in utter disbelief. The dagger has come up, and into his chest with practiced ease.

"Why?" He cannot believe how he has been killed. Mush eases him down onto one of the seats, and puts a consoling arm about his shoulders. "Oh, Mush… I…"

"Hush," Mush Draper whispers into his ear. "It will be done in a moment. You see, it was the betrayal I could not forgive. I let you inside my defences, and liked you. In time, I would have loved you, like a brother. You betrayed my friendship. I could forgive anything, except that, my dearest friend."

Digby Weller is no longer listening. His eyes glaze over, and his body relaxes. Mush eases him over the side, and into the cold water. He sits down by the tiller, and unlashes it. The rush of the river will take Digby away, and push the small boat back to the northern bank once more.

The skiff grounds, and men appear out of the darkness, and make the craft secure to the jetty. One of them is Rafe Sadler. He is about to make a stinging remark about Digby Weller's generous treatment, when he sees that Mush's doublet is stained with splashes of fresh blood. He reaches out a hand, and helps him to the shore.

"It is done," Mush says.

"I know," Rafe replies. "It is for the best. The man was far too clever to live. If he could delude us into loving him once, we might fall for it again."

"I broke my own rule," Mush says. "Trust no-one, save for the closest family. Miriam, Will, Master Tom, and you."

"I hope I will always enjoy that trust, my friend," Rafe replies, and they embrace. "We need not tell Master Cromwell what has occurred. He sought to let the man slip away, because he made the same mistake we did. He will think you did murder for him, rather than for your own reasons."

"Digby Weller took my bag of silver, and set off into the night, on foot," Mush says. "Now, I must clean up, before anyone else sees the state I am in."

"Austin Friars is empty," Rafe tells his friend. "Go there now, and I will explain your absence, by telling them all how you slipped on the bank, and became covered in mud. It will make a fine jest for the breakfast table. Mush capering about like a complete ninny; slopping around in the mud, until his finest clothes are quite ruined. Now, get yourself off!"

*

"By God, and by thunder," Henry says, as the royal barge grounds a few yards from the shore, "but your new house is a sorry sight,

Colonel Draper. The timbers are quite burnt through, and no two bricks stand upon each other. Still, what a great adventure we have had."

"My wife will be pleased," Will says, before he can stop himself.

"What, to have us back for breakfast?" Henry replies, in boisterous good spirits. He leaps from the barge, intent on splashing ashore in his manly way, and lands in a trench, scoured out by a thousand years of successive tidal shifts. The water surges up to his chest, and he gasps in horror. Will has him by the scruff of the neck, almost at once, and heaves him back into shallower water. For a moment, the king is furious, and looks to see who is laughing.

"God's teeth, Hal," Gregory guffaws, " but I swear you did that on purpose, just to lighten our mood!" Whereupon he leaps into the very spot just vacated by a furious king. "Christ on the Cross, but the water is cold!"

Henry burst into laughter, and the crew follow suit. Gregory, who is a head shorter than Henry, almost disappears, but comes up floundering. Will drags him ashore also, and slaps his back.

"A fine jest, sire, and a fine riposte, Gregory," he says, heartily. "Now we must get to a roaring fire, lest we all die of cold!"

"Well said," Henry roars. "Come on you dogs, into the water. I have not got all day!" As each hapless member of the party drops over the side, Henry roars his approval. "A fine night's hunting, Will, and a good conclusion. Why, the way we ran that fellow into the bridge, and saw off his fellow rogues, was a treat. It almost matches the time I routed the entire French army. Did I ever tell you, Colonel Will, how they tried to hold me back from the fray? I shook them off, and damned them for trying to make a coward of their king."

"They thought only to keep Your Majesty safe, sire," Will says. "Though it was ill advised to even try and stop you."

"Stop me?" Henry slaps his thigh. "I took to my horse, couched my lance, and charged. They ran after me, crying like women, as I scattered twenty thousand French knights, almost single handed!"

"The French cannot face real bravery," Gregory puts in. "Why, did not another Henry confound them once, at a place they called Agincourt?"

"By God, you are right," the king says, squelching up the shoreline. "It must be something about the name, what?"

"Very good, sire," Will says, ushering him into the hall of Draper's House. Miriam sees them enter, and sighs. The young Jewess comes forward, and takes charge. She orders blankets, hot drinks, food, and a great fire to be set, at once. Lady Jane is by her side, eagerly examining her hostesses good looking husband, standing by the stouter, muddier king.

"See," Miriam says to George Boleyn's wife, " the children have come in from their playing!"

14   Consequences

Three days have passed since the night of the great fire, and the legend has already begun to grow about the events. The court swap gossip, and then accept the version that is to become 'common knowledge' to them all. Henry, whilst visiting the Draper household, has confounded a foreign plot, and, single handed, killed three or four dangerous felons.

When asked, the king affects an air of humility, and mentions that Will Draper, and a few others did help in the adventure. No mention is made of George Boleyn's wife being on the royal barge, and no one is surprised when, with his usual generosity, Henry sends his own company of masons to help with the restoration of the burned out shell of the house.

"Such occasions lift the spirits," Henry says to Cromwell at the next meeting of the Privy Council. "Otherwise, one might end up like that dried up old stick, Norfolk."

"I fear Norfolk is old before his time," Thomas Cromwell replies. "Rafe Sadler tells me he is most vexed by his various mistresses, and that his wife is causing him more trouble. Perhaps you might consider taking some of the load from his shoulders?"

"Who else can keep order in my dockyards?"

"What about Sir Roderick Travis?" Thomas Cromwell wonders, as if the name has just entered his head. "He cannot fight on land, but he has a talent with ships."

"Do I know him?"

"He knew Martell... and hated the fellow," Cromwell explains, knowing that the king also disliked the late blackmailer, and murderer. "He was one of those felled by Colonel Draper at the joust, just before you triumphed over him."

"A damned fine bout," Henry muses. "Travis is bested by Draper, then I best him. Yes... and he disliked Martell, you say?"

"He was there when he died," Cromwell says, and taps a finger to the side of his nose.

"Ah, I see," the king says, not seeing at all. Martell ended up murdered, and he still does not quite understand how, or why. "And he is good with ships, you say?"

"Sire, you knighted him, fifteen years ago, after he sailed to the New World, and captured French and Spanish treasure ships."

"*That* Travis?" Henry's interest is aroused. "Is he the man for it still?"

"He awaits only your command, sire." Thomas Cromwell cannot believe how easily he is able to insinuate his own man into a position of power. "With the four new men o' war almost fitted out, we could put Admiral Travis in command, and have him patrol the entire Channel."

"Would that not infuriate the French?" Henry asks.

"Would it, sire?" Cromwell asks, slyly.

"Oh, you dog, Thomas," Henry says, digging him sharply in the ribs. "Ugly little Francois might even dare to send out his own navy."

"Why, yes, he might," says Thomas Cromwell. "In which case, an accomplished old corsair, like Sir Roderick Travis, might expertly dismast a few of them, and tow them all into an English port. Once re-masted, they will make a useful addition to your navy, sire. As you know, a new built ship can cost up to twenty thousand pounds. If we pay Travis a bounty of, let us say, a thousand a ship, we will save a fortune."

"See to it, Thomas," Henry whispers. "Though do not let Norfolk think that I think any the less of him."

"Of course, Your Majesty," Cromwell says. He strolls away, and circulates amongst all the others in attendance. At length he comes to Norfolk, and bows. "I am pleased to see Your Lordship is in good health."

"Why should I not be?" Norfolk asks, suspiciously.

"It is just that the king worries after your well being, My Lord."

"As he did after Sir Thomas More's?"

"Not quite, sir," Thomas Cromwell says. "He seeks only to lighten your load. It seems that he wants to give something to Sir Roderick Travis, and thinks he will make a good admiral of the Channel Fleet."

"I am the king's admiral." Norfolk stiffens, as he scents an affront, and no man in England is better at taking offence, than he.

"The king has a mind to send the fleet to Africa," Cromwell says, "or raiding along the Ottoman coasts."

"Jesus on an Ass!" Norfolk has no stomach for such a mad escapade, and suddenly does not mind being moved aside. "Though I fear that the king might flinch at insulting me so. It might be better if... yes, I will resign ... due to ill health. Then again, what if he keeps the fleet at home?"

"He may not."

"But I am the admiral of the fleet!"

"You *were,* sir," Thomas Cromwell says, shrugging his shoulders. "I did plead your case, somewhat, but his mind is made up. Odd really."

"What is?"

"He seemed happy enough with you, when last we talked," Cromwell says. "Then, he is allowed a visit with his confined wife, and ... well, it may be nothing, but ..."

"That cow!" Norfolk spits. "She seeks to put me aside for one of her favourites, now she is queen!"

"Hardly that," Thomas Cromwell replies. "Why, what reason would she have to do that? Although, Admiral Travis is quite friendly with her father, I hear."

"I will not have it." Norfolk snaps. "I will see the king, at once."

"And tell him what?" Thomas Cromwell asks. "That your niece wants rid of you? Why, he might put you aside, just so she is not upset. The king is placing a lot on the coming birth."

"Then what should I do?" Norfolk asks. He is like a rudderless ship, ever since his confederate, Suffolk withdrew from court, claiming ill health.

"Hold your peace." Cromwell beckons to Rafe Sadler. "Let yourself be guided by Master Sadler. He has no love for the Boleyns, and will warn you, if anything more occurs. He will also let you know when it is time."

"Time?"

"To strike, sir." Cromwell says. "What else can you do when a poisonous snake comes at you? The head must be cut off."

"Have a care, Cromwell," the duke says. "You speak of the queen."

"Do I?" Thomas Cromwell asks. "I speak only of protecting oneself from a dangerous creature."

"Of course." Norfolk nods to Rafe. "Be my man then, Sadler, and I am grateful for it."

"Sir," Rafe Sadler bows. "You do well to step aside. Henry means to provoke the French navy. If the fleet fights, and loses, there must be certain consequences. Heads will roll, if he loses, and if he wins… you can claim it is because of your prior good husbandry of the fleet."

"Clever fellow," Norfolk says. "Come, we will speak more."

"Much, and often, sir," Rafe says, as they stroll off, towards the gardens.

*

"Are you still here, waiting to speak to the king, dear Eustace?" Thomas Cromwell asks his friend, as he leaves the council chamber.

"I am, Thomas. I wish permission to visit the queen."

"The queen?" Cromwell raises an eyebrow. "She is abed, and with child, sir."

"The Dowager Princess of Wales then," Eustace Chapuys replies. "The lady who many still think of as the rightful wife of King Henry. She is very unwell, and I fear for her life."

"Seriously, old friend?"

"Since Arch Bishop Cranmer forced through the divorce, Katherine's health has been declining. She spends most of her time in prayer, hoping the king will come to his senses."

"She prays for Queen Anne to die in childbirth, and for the baby to be stillborn."

"That is outrageous, Thomas," Chapuys says. "How can you say such a thing?"

"I have it written down. A detailed report from one of her ladies-in-waiting; that she does *curse* the queen, and *prays* for her death, daily." Cromwell sighs. "I cannot allow her to spread her vile poison further a field. Nor can I allow you a private visit, at this time."

"What if…" The ambassador is thinking of the dangers of childbirth, and wishes to put forward a hypothesis.

"Do not say it, Ambassador Chapuys!" Cromwell's tone becomes sharp, and his face freezes into a stone like expression. "To even think it is treason. I would have to denounce you, and have you sent back to your emperor, in disgrace."

"Then I will not say it," Chapuys tells his friend. "Though I wonder what outcome will suit you the best, old friend?"

"I go with the tide, Eustace," Cromwell answers. "For whatever happens, there are consequences. I pray you, do not petition the king today. Flatter him, compare him favourably to a lion, and tell him a funny story."

"I do not understand English humour."

Chapuys knows when he is beaten, and shelves any hope of seeing Katherine in the near future.

"Tell him the new one that Tom Wyatt is putting about."

"And what is that?"

"Why about the fellow who asks Wyatt if he be as great a wit as folk make out. Tom Wyatt says he is, and can pun on any subject the fellow might name. Whereupon the wily man says '*the king*' to Wyatt, and the poet simply smiles at him, and says… '*but kind sir, the king is not a fit subject!*' It will have him roaring his head off."

"I do not understand," Chapuys says. "The king is not a subject… he is the king."

"Just use the jest." Cromwell moves off, hoping to catch Stephen Gardiner, the Archbishop of Winchester. They were once good friends, and he seeks to win him back. Gardiner, for his part, wishes to stay sitting on the fence.

"Good day, Stephen."

"No, Master Cromwell," Archbishop Gardiner says, as he attempts to sidestep his old friend. "I cannot see my way to coming down your road just yet."

"We all need friends, even the Bishop of Winchester," Cromwell replies. "If you must sit on your high fence, then let me caution you. Do not come down from it… ever … lest you land on the wrong side!"

"Good day, Cromwell," Gardiner says. He affects a slight bow, and moves off into the outer chambers.

"Seeking allies, Thomas?" Archbishop Cranmer asks, as he comes out from the king.

"Henry tells me that you, and that ass, George Boleyn, have fallen out over something. Can you not see your way to forgive him?"

"Why not, for the king has." Thomas Cromwell shakes his head, sadly. "He has his new wife now, Cranmer, and little need for us. We must shift for ourselves, lest we be swept away, like poor old Tom More."

"Was it not you who did for Sir Thomas More?" Cranmer asks, sarcastically.

"I had him retire, to save his life."

"Well, it was to no avail. The king has told me to go to him, and demand that he take the oath."

"God's teeth!" Cromwell cannot believe it. "Why not leave the fellow to his own devices?"

"Consequences," Archbishop Cranmer mutters. "Let More refuse, and half of England will follow suit, or so Queen Anne keeps on saying to the king."

"That is a great nonsense."

"Henry listens to her more than his ministers," the archbishop replies. "Once the child comes, she will become quite insufferable."

"She raised you to your current position," Thomas Cromwell reminds him. "Are you not her creature?"

"I am God's creature, sir, and I seek to bring the light of His knowledge into England. A bible, in every church, written in English. She seeks the wealth of Rome, so that she might aggrandise herself in His eyes." Cranmer snaps back.

"Ah, then it all about the treasure, after all," Thomas Cromwell says. "It is not to do with the church, but with its vile wealth. This coming year, I will milk almost a million pounds from the Roman faith in England, and would spend it on great works."

"More new war ships?" Cranmer says.

"With England safe, its people will become freer, and this land will prosper, like no other," says Cromwell. "Queen Anne will have her way, and dole out the wealth to only those who worship at her alter."

"You throw caution to the winds, sir," Cranmer tells him. "If she hears of this, she will…"

"Destroy me?" Thomas Cromwell chuckles. "Let her try. Brother George has had his chance, and failed. Thomas Boleyn has tried, and lost his way. They will find that a blacksmith's lad can be even harder to bring down than the son of an Ipswich butcher. It took them all to fell Cardinal Wolsey."

"But he fell, nevertheless."

"As have his enemies," Cromwell replies. "Where is Harry Percy? The Duke of Northumberland has not shown his face in council for many a long month. The Boleyns, father and son, are under a cloud, and even Norfolk is being edged out. The curse of Wolsey is powerful indeed."

"Then I am glad I never crossed the fellow." Archbishop Cranmer wishes nothing now, but a quiet life. He too would like to sit on Bishop Stephen Gardiner's wall, but he doubts there is enough room for more than one coward.

Colonel Will Draper is helping to peg out bed sheets with his wife, and two of the many servant girls in their employ. He is in his shirt sleeves, and must help hold up the wet bedding, so that the girls can fix it on the long rope clothes lines, with carved wooden pegs.

"I promised Tom Wyatt to meet him later," he grumbles, only to receive a glowering look from Miriam. "Not for drinking," he continues. "He has an idea to publish a book of his poems, and wishes my advice."

"Wishes your money, more like," Miriam says. "How much does he want?"

"Four hundred pounds," Will admits.

"For how many prints?"

"He thought a hundred."

"Then he must sell every one for five pounds, just to make a tiny profit," Miriam says. "Why does he not ask Master Cromwell?"

"Miriam, it is only four hundred pounds."

"Very well, but I must have control of the outlay. I wish to see the copy, and approve it. I will not spend hundreds and hundreds, on lilting love lyrics. His poems must be bawdy, and come across as quite rude."

"What?" Will can scarcely believe what she says. "You *want* him to write … filth?"

"It is all that will sell well," Miriam says. "Why, even your Holy Bible, when printed in English, must be *given* away to the churches. I shall invest five hundred, and expect two hundred volumes. At five pounds a turn, we will make a tidy profit, which we will split in half."

"I do not know if Wyatt knows enough bawd

to fill a book."

"It need not have too many pages," Miriam replies. "In fact, the fewer the better. That will keep costs down. Brother Mush, and Master Cromwell's agents can start putting out a rumour that the book is so saucy, the churchmen wish it to be banned. Let it be known that it describes great men swiving, and young courtly tarts simpering away their virginity."

"Good God, what have I married?"

"Hints and promises, my dear." Miriam winks at him across the wet sheets. "That way, it will sell out more quickly."

"You are a marvel, my love," Will says. "Do you never take a rest from making money for us?"

"I dare not," Miriam says. "Especially now, when there is going to be another mouth to feed."

"What, more guests?" Will Draper, the king's best investigator takes a moment for it to sink home, then gasps in astonishment. "Again, and so soon?"

"I cannot think what is causing it," Miriam says. "Will you still love me, when I grow fat again?"

"More than ever," Will says. "This one shall be called Thomas, I think."

"Or Thomasina," Miriam says. "Master Cromwell will be honoured, either way."

Will Draper can think of nothing better than another little Draper in the world. They are making more money than anyone can imagine, and are known, and liked, by the king. The new house, despite the recent arson attack, is going back up at a pace, and Miriam is introducing the most modern amenities into the design, much to the disgust of the builder, who cannot see the point of a fixed bath, when it would be used no more than three of four times a year. Nor could the poor fellow understand the need for tiled privies, with separate stalls.

"We are close to the river," Miriam explains, time after time to the master builder and his men. "We will draw water into the house. I want a tank built, with an oven underneath it. My girls will stoke a fire, and heat water, for all the day long use."

"It cannot be done." The builder is, of course, wrong. Miriam Draper has been reading in Cromwell's library, and has the facts at her pretty fingertips.

"The Romans did it," she says.

"They be dead, and long gone."

"The Ottomans do it," Miriam says, "and they are nothing more than heathens, are they not?"

"Even the king does not have such a thing."

"Then he should have," Miriam says to them. "Do this for me, and I will speak to my husband, who will speak to Henry, and the king will want exactly the same, but thirty fold. I shall recommend you, sir, and you will prosper."

"Righto, lads," the fellow says, at last. "Let us start work. If this fine lady wishes to shit in private, then so be it!"

*

The big, broadly built mariner is sitting in

the hall of Austin Friars, when Cromwell returns. He stands, and bows, then offers his hand to shake.

"Master Cromwell, I believe I have you to thank for my new commission, and come to offer you my friendship. If ever I can be of some service to you, in any way... you have but to ask."

"Excellent." Thomas Cromwell ushers Admiral Travis into his library. "How do you feel about bombarding Tangiers for me, old fellow?"

"Tangiers?" Travis is taken by surprise. "Why would you wish me to do such a thing, Master Cromwell?"

"Gonçalo Mendes Sacoto, has just been appointed Governor of Tangiers, by the Portuguese." Cromwell offers the admiral a seat by the fire. "They are allies of ours, but waver between us, and the French, in their struggle to keep the Spanish at bay."

"So, you want me to capture Tangiers?" Travis is confused.

"Good heavens, no," Cromwell explains. "I wish you to sail past the harbour, and fire a few cannonades against their walls."

"It will do no harm," the sailor advises. "The fortifications would need to be pounded for weeks."

"I do not want any *harm* done," Thomas Cromwell says. "Simply blow a few chunks out of the masonry, and sail off. Though you must be flying French colours at the time."

"I see," Travis laughs. "The Portuguese will waver, until the French bombard Tangiers."

"Precisely. They will ratify the treaty, at once, and ask for our help in defending their overseas possessions. The king will agree, and we will threaten the French with retaliation. They will protest their innocence… but that is what one expects. Henry will demand we build more ships, and let you loose along the Channel ports."

"Then you seek war?"

"The opposite," Cromwell says. "I seek to rob a lady of the money she needs to ruin me." The king will start to think about arming England, and he will need every penny he can lay his hands on. The church confiscations will go into ship building, rather than Queen Anne's purse. "France will not fight over a colony they do not actually want. They might try to raid our coast, but I am sure you can handle that. The king will pay a bounty for captured French warships … which we will split."

"Halves?"

"Of course, Admiral Travis."

"When do I sail?" the admiral asks.

"Soon," Cromwell tells his new ally. "I await only a certain piece of news."

*

"Father, come to bed, it is late," Margaret Roper says, touching Sir Thomas More's shoulder. He starts, and almost drops the parchment he has balanced on his knee.

"I cannot yet, daughter," he says. Return to Roper, and be a goodly wife to him. I shall speak with you both tomorrow."

"You read the document over and over, father," Margaret says. "The words will not change."

"But their meaning might," More replies, rubbing his weary eyes. "If I can find one chink of light, I can use it to confound this prurient oath."

Margaret leaves him then. She has read the draft of the Supreme Oath until it is fixed in her mind, and she cannot yet see a way around the clever wording. Rafe Sadler, Thomas Cromwell, and the rest of Henry's fine lawyers, have done good job.

"I Margaret Roper do utterly testify, and declare, in my conscience, that the Kings Highness is the only Supreme Governor of this Realm," she mutters to herself, *"and all other of His Highnesses dominions and countries, as well in all spiritual, or ecclesiastical things or causes."* She ponders over this part, which grants the king sway over the church in England. *"And that no foreign prince, person, prelate, State, or potentate, hath, or ought to have, any jurisdiction, power, superiorities, pre-eminence, or ecclesiastical or spiritual authority, within this Realm."*

She recognises that the foreign princes alluded to include, pre-eminently, Pope Clement, in Rome, and any other who may ever follow him into office.

"And therefore, I do utterly renounce, and forsake, all jurisdictions, powers, or authorities; and do promise that from henceforth I shall bear faithful, and true allegiance to the Kings Highness, his Heirs, and lawful successors," she finishes. *"and to my power shall assist, and defend, all that belongs to the king. So help me God."*

Every single exit is, seemingly, blocked, and

every road leads back to that one, central question. My God, or my king? The oath puts duty to one's king above duty to God, and even suggests that the two are indivisible. Margaret Roper knows, no matter how he reads it, that her father will never be able to take the great oath.

He will argue his case, and repel all attempts to sway him, but they will have their way in the end. Even if Thomas Cromwell, that most unlikely ally, moves as slowly as he can get away with, the end is inevitable. Within twelve, or eighteen months, her father will be condemned to death, for treason.

She slips back into her husband's bed, and he enfolds her in his arms. She begins to weep. He squeezes her tighter to him.

"I know, my dearest one," he says. "I know."

Back in his chair by the dwindling fire, Sir Thomas More reads the oath through once more.

"Just one misplaced word, dear God, and I will argue them to a standstill," he mutters. "My eyes grow weary. Show me the way, O Lord, that I might come into the grace of God, and confound those who would pervert your word."

*

"Where is Brandon?" Henry's casual question causes a flurry of reactions, and Thomas Cromwell is sent for, to give the king his answer. The Privy Councillor arrives at Whitehall Palace, armed with several good reasons why the Duke of Suffolk is absent at this time. Henry will have none of them.

"Ill, you say?" the king asks shaking his head. "Charles has never had a moment's illness that I know of, and that would not keep him away from his dearest friend. There is a deeper reason, I fear, Master Cromwell, and I would have it, at once."

"His Lordship might be out of sorts because of Your Highnesses own current good fortune," Cromwell extemporises. In truth, he has thrown Brandon out of court, as a punishment for his recent attempt at stealing from the treasury, but dare not admit it.

"What, he resents me?" Henry is beginning to colour up, and his fists are clenching and unclenching.

"Never, sire!" Thomas Cromwell puts on his shocked expression. "It is just that he lost his dear wife … your sister … and you are about to become a father again. Perhaps he does not wish to mope about court, and ruin your happiness."

"Ah, that is just like Charles. Noble to the last. Can a man ever have had a better friend, Thomas?"

"Indeed not, sire." Cromwell sees what is coming, so uses it to make himself look better in Henry's eyes. "Though his nobility of thought is misplaced. His duty is to be by the king's side, during these last days of the queen's confinement. His nobility might be misinterpreted as sulking by lesser men, such as…"

"Say it, Thomas, say it!" Henry wants someone to blame for his current state of boredom.

"The Earl of Wiltshire can be a little … over sensitive, sire," Cromwell says. "Then again,

George, whom you have forgiven for his attack against you..."

"Against *me*?" Henry is confused.

"Why yes, sire. He sought to do damage to your Official Examiner, which constitutes an attack on the king. He is fortunate indeed, as to whom his sister is."

"Yes, the Boleyns take far too much for granted," Henry says. "I want Charles back in court. Suffolk is my friend. Then find some little way that I might slight Boleyn, and his idiot son. Nothing too harsh, for I would not upset the queen for all the world."

"Now you mention it, sire... there is one thing." Thomas Cromwell cannot believe his luck at how easily he can use that which Rafe Sadler has just brought to his attention. "One of your people came to me, but this morning, worried that a royal prerogative has been usurped."

"How so?"

"Wiltshire, Your Majesty." Cromwell explains. "It seems that there has never been a previous Earl of Wiltshire. Now, whenever the king decides to create an entirely new dukedom, it is *his* prerogative to appoint the holder."

"Naturally." Henry understands this well enough, as no king would allow lesser men to choose his earls, or dukes, for him. In the past, English kings have been served badly, by those with too much power. It is Henry's maxim that he will bestow position where it is deserved, but not too much, and not too often. "As the father of my wife, Thomas Boleyn should have an earldom, which will devolve onto George, his idiot son."

"As it should be, sire, but it is the custom for those chosen, to pay an *enfeoffment* to the king, to show his loyalty." Thomas Cromwell raises a finger to his lips, as if he finds this talk of huge wealth to be a little distasteful to him. "Your man showed me the rules, concerning these very rare, and wonderful, endowments. They are enshrined in our laws, and date from the time of the first King William."

"William the Bastard, they used to call the fellow," Henry digresses. "Though he must have been a fearsome wager of war. I have his blood in me, no doubt."

"Quite, sire." Cromwell pauses, waits for the king to settle again, then continues. "The amount due, can vary from one tenth, up to a full quarter part of the estate's overall value."

"I say!" Henry is smiling now. He glances across the throne room, and sees Thomas Boleyn, 1st Earl of Wiltshire, chatting to Sir Edward Crompton, who acts as the king's chief lackey, whenever The Duke of Suffolk is away. "This might be a merry jest to make, Thomas. Have him over."

Thomas Cromwell bows, and whispers to Rafe Sadler, who bows in return, and goes across the room, to fetch Thomas Boleyn from his small corner. The Earl of Wiltshire sees Rafe coming towards him, and turns his back, slightly, as if to exclude him from any conversation. Rafe Sadler does not even pause. He taps the man, quite rudely, on the shoulder, and plucks at his sleeve, until the earl is forced to acknowledge him.

"The king would have a word, Boleyn," he

says, roughly, and the earl can hardly control his rage. About him, people have noticed the deliberate insult, and are beginning to snigger and laugh at him, behind their cupped hands. "At once!"

"Keep your hands to yourself, fellow," Boleyn snaps, but not loud enough for the king to hear. "Else my *cousin* will hear of it."

"Your cousin, who is also your son-in-law?" Rafe Sadler sneers. "What a complicated family tree for any dog to sniff around, sir. I think that you have more to worry about than I do. Whilst I think on it, Master Cromwell's first repayment is due at month's end. Three thousand four hundred pounds, and some shillings, I believe. See you do not renege on it … *fellow*." He walks away, forcing Thomas Boleyn to fall in behind, like some naughty child, going to the head master.

"Master Cromwell, here is the earl," Rafe says to his old master. "As you commanded."

"Ah, yes. Your Majesty, here is Thomas Boleyn, as *you* commanded."

"My title is *My Lord*." Boleyn cannot refrain from protecting his public stature. He sees himself as but a step down from Henry, and many steps above the likes of Thomas Cromwell. Only Tom Howard, Duke of Norfolk, has a higher opinion of himself, and he sees the throne as his family's entitlement.

"It seems not," the king says, chuckling. "For you have not yet paid me an *enfeoffment*, my dear father-in-law. You do know what an *enfeoffment* is, do you not, father-in-law? Dear Master Cromwell tells me that it is now customary, nay ... statutory ... in such cases."

"Customary?" Thomas Boleyn senses some awful new trick is being played on him, and cannot understand how his life has taken so poor a turn, of late. It is as if all the hobgoblins in Hell are conspiring to make his existence as difficult as they can.

"I fear so, Master Boleyn," Cromwell says, and Henry actually laughs out loud. He has no intention of imposing the due, and merely wishes to make a jest of it. Then Cromwell continues. "It will, of course, be set at the lowest figure... for the king loves you as a father ... of a tithe."

"Yes, a tithe," Henry says, winking at his Privy Councillor.

"Which, at current land values, taking into account the huge flocks of sheep thereon, and the virgin woodlands, will amount to some ... three hundred thousand pounds."

"Good Christ!" Henry is no longer smiling. He lurches forward on his throne, and stabs a thick finger at his cowering father-in-law. "You thought to grant *yourself* title to my own dear county of Wiltshire ... without any recompense to the treasury?"

"Sire... I did not know!" Boleyn is stuttering. "This is the first I have heard of the matter. Why, Charles Brandon was made the 1st Earl of Suffolk, was he not?"

"My Lord Suffolk was assessed at the time, sire," Rafe Sadler puts in. "As he *offered* a tenth portion, without being pushed, Your Majesty allowed him to settle over a ten year period. Besides, his county was not so highly priced back then. The debt is long discharged."

"Three hundred thousand pounds?" Henry looks from Cromwell to Sadler, and settles on Boleyn. "You shall have the same terms as Charles, who you are so quick to condemn, Boleyn. Ten years, at thirty thousand a year."

"With interest, sire?" Rafe Sadler asks, softly.

"Why not?" Henry's jest has fallen flat, but results in him being many thousands of pounds richer for it. "Though only from today's date, I think."

"The seventh day of September, sire... as you command."

"Sire!" Sir Edward Crompton is at the throne room's door, with a young pageboy standing his side. He sees that all eyes are upon him. "News, at last!"

Thomas Boleyn knows, at once, what it is, and sees a swift forgiveness on the horizon. He turns, and sneers at Thomas Cromwell, whose face is adopting a waxen hue.

"To the winner, the spoils," Boleyn mutters to Cromwell. "Now you will dance to my tune, blacksmith's boy!"

"Well, what is it?" Henry towers from his throne, and throws his arms out wide. "Tell me!"

"Sire," Sir Edward Crompton announces. "You are a father, and the queen is well."

"Must I strangle the bastard?" Henry cries. "Speak, fellow!"

"Your Majesty has ... a *daughter*."

Thomas Cromwell sees the look on the king's face, and the horror of the news sends

Boleyn reeling back. He snatches at Rafe Sadler's sleeve, and draws him to one side, urgently.

"By God, Rafe, the bitch has failed," Cromwell says. "Get word to Austin Friars, at once. Have our people start whispering about how the king is cursed. Spare no expense. We will have but one chance at this, and must take it. Before another twelve months are gone, we will be ruined, or have ruined Anne Boleyn."

"Yes, master." Rafe slips away, whilst the entire court stands about, cowering in silence. The need for a son was so palpably felt by all, that no one can think what to say. It is Thomas Cromwell who breaks the silence. To the shock of all, he mounts the low dais that supports the throne, and throws his arms around the king. There is an audible gasp from the throng at such an outrageous act.

"Sire, do not show dismay, I beg of you," he whispers into Henry's ear. "You are the king, and must not show weakness to these people. It is a small setback, and one, as virile as the king, shall soon sire many more children ... of both sexes. Understood?"

The king tries to pull away at first, until Cromwell's words sink into his mind. Slowly, he relaxes, and allows Cromwell to finish what he must say. Then Cromwell steps back, and bows to his king.

"Thomas Cromwell, you are my rock, once more." Henry nods his complete understanding.

"Forgive my forwardness, sire," Cromwell says, still bowing. "I was overcome with pleasure at the news. Your daughter is healthy, and your queen lives!"

"Thank you, Master Cromwell," Henry says. "I have often heard that a filly seldom foals a stallion, first time. Let me but regain my vigour, and I will fill these halls with children's voices."

"God save the king, Queen Anne, and the new princess!" Thomas Cromwell shouts, and the room erupts into wild cheers.

*

"He said that?" Queen Anne is tired from her labours, yet must have all the court news, from those closest to her. The reports are coming in fast, and she must sort the clever wheat from the banal chaff. "He actually likened me to a horse?"

"A fine filly, sister," George Boleyn says. "In that we do both heartily concur."

"And what about Cromwell?"

"He had them all crying 'God save Henry, and Queen Anne', out loud," a lady in waiting puts in. "Then he actually blesses the new princess."

"Cromwell was first to praise me?" Anne Boleyn smiles, and nods her head. "Then I must be most careful. For by this, he means to ingratiate himself with my husband. We must make our move soon, father. Cromwell is the real enemy."

"That he is," the Earl of Wiltshire says. "He hems me in on all sides, and seeks to lessen my power over Henry."

"He is a clever man," George mutters. "Let us hope you have enough time to bring forth a son, before he acts!"

"Let him," Queen Anne says. "Henry has a

child by me now, and cannot think of putting me aside. Even his own church will not countenance that. No, I must bring him to my bed once more."

"Is he up to it?" George asks.

"Clear the room," Anne snaps. "I would talk with my brother, alone." The elder Boleyn, and all of the ladies in waiting leave, and George moves to sit by his sister.

"Will you stay by me, George?" she asks.

"I will."

"Do you remember when we were a little younger?" Anne asks. "Me, you, sister Mary, and Tom Wyatt, playing in the meadow, at Hever Castle?"

"Of course."

"Good. Then, if I call upon your services…"

"Enough, sister," George replies. He kisses her on the forehead, and runs a finger down her cheek, to her lips. "One glance from you, and I am ready. Did ever a brother love his sister so much?"

"We must be discreet," Anne says. "Should Henry not be man enough, then I *will* seek other means."

"Your servant, Your Majesty," George says, and smiles, as he remembers times past. "To the very end!"

~end~

Afterword

The incestuous relationship between Anne Boleyn, and her brother, George is, almost certainly a fiction. Though the two grew up together, and had a close bond, there is no supporting evidence for the claims. I use the possibility, merely as a fictional ploy, with which to embellish my story. There is also little evidence to suggest that George was either a homosexual, or a bi-sexual. Tudor views of these vices are ambiguous, and official stances vary from those held in private. Like the later Victorian age, the Tudors did not mind, providing that it went on behind closed doors.

My fictional alchemist, Aldo Mercurius, is a distillation of many in Tudor times, who claimed magical, or alchemical powers. The story of the Philosopher's Stone is widely known, and usually alludes to the turning of base metals into pure gold. In fact, most of the better alchemists (the scientists and chemists of the day) sought to create elixirs to cure illnesses, or prolong life.

I must apologise, yet again, for the varying interpretations I make of historic figures. Though I am sure my portrayal of Henry is close to the mark. His various disorders made him ever more unreliable in later life, and prone to listen to whom ever wished to whisper in his ear.

Suffolk was a commoner, who had the luck (good or bad) to be made a playmate of Henry, as a child. He grew into the perfect courtier, and figured throughout many of Henry's darkest moments.

Norfolk was a survivor, and it is easy to see how he can move from one allegiance to another, without the benefit of conscience. As the first noble of England, he was able to support the reformation of the English church, yet remain a Roman Catholic, in private.

During Queen Anne's progression from the wedding ceremony, the king noted how the crowds cheered for him, yet turned away from his queen, and even catcalled to her. From the first, he was aware of the peoples strong feelings, yet pressed on, knowing that a son would solve every ill.

As we know, Queen Anne produced Elizabeth, a daughter, and only entangled the royal couple in further constitutional discord. The great oath is almost upon the general public, and soon, Sir Thomas More, and many others must make their minds up. Their king, or their faith?

As for Thomas Cromwell, and his young men at Austin Friars, there is a rocky road ahead. The queen is against him, and it is up to him to unravel the Gordian Knot that is English politics. Can he untie the intricate bond, or must he cut it through, and see where the pieces fall?

Anne Stevens.

Coming Soon....

A Twilight of Queens

In this, the eighth volume of the Tudor Crimes series, we see the final struggle between Thomas Cromwell, and Queen Anne. Having helped to bring down one queen, Cromwell is compelled to go against another, more powerful consort. The King sways, like a rowan tree in the wind, waiting for his secret wishes to be fulfilled.

Anne Boleyn holds the fate of England in her two hands, and struggles to give the king the one thing which he most craves - a son. Even as Cromwell, and Anne, prepare for the final conflict, Henry is about to throw everything into turmoil, because of one small whim. In a dangerous age, one smile, and the touch of a hand can change a country's future, forever.

Whilst the great and the good clash, the life of everyday Tudor England must go on apace. Whilst the king wants a son, his people want nothing more than a full stomach, and a quiet life.

Will Draper, now a Colonel of the King's Horse, and head of the King's Royal Examiners, is to become a father again, and must face up to his investigative duties, aided by a new recruit... John Beckshaw, a no nonsense Yorkshire born, young man.

Together, they must investigate the terrible case of a fabled beast, roaming the countryside, and solve the intriguing riddle of a self confessed witch.

Miriam Draper makes her first trip to France, in search of new trade opportunities, and finds something quite different. Mush continues to struggle along in a world that is not his, and returns to a lost love, where he will find nothing but heartache.

The very fabric of Tudor England is about to be ripped apart, and Thomas Cromwell must search his own conscience, before embarking on a terrible mission. Something has to give, and the inhabitants of Austin Friars do not want it to be them, or their way of life.

For her part, Anne Boleyn, Queen of England, and mother of the infant Princess Elizabeth must take a dangerous course, if she is to have a chance of ultimate success. She gambles everything, to win for her family, the greatest prize of all - the throne of England.

Book 8 ~ A Twilight of Queens ~ will be out in the Spring of 2016

What do the critics think?

Writing about 'The King's Angels' critical reviewer A Boffin says: "This series goes from strength to strength and I await the next slice of Cromwell ... I cannot wait for my Tudor fix!"

"I have just finished reading this [The Condottiero]. The plot, and the main character smacks of Hercule Poirot ... a good read!" C J Parsons, UK Reviews.

A reader of 'The Condottiero' writes "Another Tudor winner .... A big, sprawling epic that encompasses a dizzying array of characters. Number four in the series, and already is up to the writing of Maurice Druon's 'Accursed Kings' series, the works of Alfred Duggan, and G R R Mason's Game of Thrones."

"A welcome addition to the genre ... Anne Stevens writes with an urgency that keeps the pages turning..." ....Bel Ami.

"I didn't want it to finish...." Amazon reader [about Midnight Queen.]

5 out of 5 stars from: Swan2 [Winter King.]
'I love the Shardlake series and it reminded me a bit of them. A good read for the holidays ... though I worked out the killer quite early on!'

5 stars 24 Jun. 2015: By Amazon Customer: 'Brilliant, I enjoyed every bit of it !'

5 stars, posted 28 Oct. 2015 by C. J. Parsons Kindle Edition Verified Purchase
'A gripping read... well written.'

<u>Customer Reviews of 'Midnight Queen'</u>

5.0 out of 5 stars. 24 Jun. 2015 by Amazon Customer / Kindle edition.

'Excellent read ,cannot wait for next one...'

4.0 out of 5 stars, posted on 14th Oct. 2015 by Maureen Price Format:Kindle Edition | Verified Purchase : "Didn't want it to end"

4.0 out of 5 stars <u>Good read</u> [17 Nov. 2015]… by Loopy Loo *
"I thoroughly enjoyed this. It makes easy reading, and flows well. I look forward to the next book in 2016."

* The King's Examiner

5 stars. Good read… very interesting. Couldn't put the book down until I reached the end of it. Good characterisation, and plots. Sharon McAndrew's review on Amazon.

Thank you all for the above reviews. In this crazy world, the more reviews we get, the better the algorithms (?), which means we get promoted by Amazon better. What ever happened to poor old Bill Posters … was he finally prosecuted?

TightCircle Publications are a small publishing house, who rely entirely on sales through Amazon. We hope you enjoyed this book, and recommend it to a friend. A good review also helps sales, and increased sales help keep our costs down so we can continue to sell to the reading public at a fair price.
The author and publishers hold the soul rights to the publication, dissemination, and printing of these books, by whatever means is available. The intellectual property rights remain with the author, and no part should, without permission, ever be quoted, re-printed, e-mailed or in any other way promoted, without the express written permission of the owner.

© TightCircle Publications & Author

This book (print edition) is dedicated to everyone who has supported me since the concept of a great Tudor saga first came to me. My partner, editors, friends, supporters, and promotors have all contributed to the huge effort, and I can only thank them, one and all.

My thanks must also go to all involved with F11 ... you know who you are.

Printed in Great Britain
by Amazon